TRUE WIND

This book is a work of fiction.

All characters and events are the products of the author's imagination.

The story is part of a series but stands alone.

Series Titles

WHITE COLLAR OPTION

THEN GO STRAIGHT FORWARD

WAITING FOR THE STORM TO PASS

THEIR WILL BE DONE

POINTED INWARDS

MADE TO ACCOUNT

CHAIN REACTION

CONSIGNMENT

TRUE WIND

The author has been a journalist for more than 30 years; among the many news outlets for which he has worked are The Times, Observer, the BBC and UPI. He has taught journalism in the UK and USA.

He was born in Glasgow, Scotland but lived for many years in Washington, DC and Florida where this story is located.

Thanks to family and friends for their support which made this book possible.

Special thanks to Rosamund for her encouragement, patience and diligent proofreading.

Additional thanks to Di and Ian Cormack, Bob Meek and Steve Murray, whose critical eyes help spot the errors which may have got away.

Thanks again to my pal Barney for keeping me company while I searched for the words.

Preface

St. Augustine, Florida

The gin-palace barflies, the social leeches and the drunks had finally called it a day, dragging their inebriated bodies ashore. The cacophony had abated and a ghostly silence descended on the estuary. The yacht pulled on its anchor, creaking quietly in rhythm with the surrounding sea. The diver waited long enough to ensure it was clear.

The darkness enveloped him as he slid silently into the water from the shore. It was calm, devoid of even a breath, the wind barely making any impact on the rows of the anchored, costly and coveted sailboats. The toys of the rich and carefree gently bobbed up and down like corks in a barrel, as if jostling with each other, straining the assortment of ropes that kept them in place. Ripples from the diver's snorkel were scarcely visible, just tiny circles whose edges reflected the occasional flash of light from the harbour.

It was not the first time he'd stolen an expensive yacht. He was one of the modern nautical thieves responsible for stealing hundreds each year, some to order, but always for profit. So far, the night had gone as planned.

A minute later the diver was in the shadows beside the hull of the yacht, moored about a hundred yards from the shore. It was difficult for him to see the deck from the waterline. Confident that there was no one on board, he pulled away from the craft to get a better view then surfaced. There was no sign of life.

In less than a minute he had climbed one of the side ladders, quickly hauled himself on deck, removed his snorkel and slipped his head out of the wetsuit. He listened intently. A few voices wafted their way across the water from the shore. There was no other sound. Once more he carefully scoured the deck for any sign of life, and listened; again nothing.

He knew what to do. He had done it many times. The ropes holding the yacht to the moorings offered little challenge. He cut through them quickly with the tool he had strapped to his waist. He used another to silently break into the cabin.

The tide was on the turn. That was part of the plan. He felt the craft drift slowly, jettison its ties and silently slip from its moorings. He switched off all its mooring lights and let it drift invisible, cloaked in the darkness, aided by the current out of the harbour. The covered moon offered little brightness and the odd beam of light which escaped from the shore started to fade into the distance as the yacht moved into open water. The craft picked up more speed with the current and shot into the darkness. Ten minutes later the diver had shorted an electrical circuit and fired up the engine; part one of the job complete.

Chapter 1

St. Augustine, Florida

The bruised face of a man in his sixties appeared as the policeman pulled back the green cover from the corpse on the trolley. The blanched and pimpled skin of the hideous human sculpture made the tattoos on each of the forearms more prominent, although the writing on them had faded and was barely decipherable. The words stretched from the wrists to the shoulders like a biblical scroll. McCabe, journalist, hovering several feet away, squinted at the words and mimed them slowly as he read.

The text said something about *God* and the *Sea*; a maritime prayer that sounded vaguely familiar, if not clichéd. That was as much as he could see. McCabe moved closer and peered at the wording again just as the smell of the corpse hit him; not the odour of death that he'd expected or the hint of the formaldehyde that enveloped most of the forensic room but a waft of something else he couldn't identify. It was sickly and nauseating.

'Where was he found?' he asked, slowly moving further forward, almost cautiously.

Pete Fischer, Police Chief of St. Augustine, the idyllic waterfront town in eastern Florida, moved closer to the body too but said nothing in reply. He walked round the corpse quietly, studying the tattoo. 'Ugly, isn't it,' he said, examining the markings closely. 'I mean the tattoo,' he added quickly as if correcting himself. 'They never did much for me, although I'm told they're getting popular again,' he said, pulling the cover sheet further down the body. 'But it does help in identification, normally.'

'Normally?' quizzed McCabe, still looking uncomfortable.

'Yes, but not in this case; we have you now,' the policeman added with a smile. The expression was more of a reflex than any attempt at warmth. It was sardonic by anyone's definition. McCabe stared at the corpse again but still a few cautious feet away. He seemed reluctant to move any closer, as if not wanting to play any part in the proceedings. He still looked uncomfortable, an unhappy spectator who was being dragged onto the stage. 'You didn't give me much choice.' The words shot across the room. The hollow acoustics made them sound louder than he'd expected. 'Two uniformed policemen marched me from my hotel room,' he continued with a detectable edge to his voice. 'It could hardly be described as an invitation, however polite the persuasion.'

'Marched?' repeated the policeman. 'You guys do like to exaggerate, don't you?' he added quickly. His voice had changed in tone. The resonance had suddenly got harsher. 'You were invited to help the police with their enquiries,' said the policeman very slowly, without even a hint of apology. The cold contrived smile appeared again.

'I must have missed that subtle nuance,' commented McCabe, the bitterness in his voice still evident. 'MARCHED is the perfect description,' he insisted, emphasising the word, defending its use. He was annoyed and his voice conveyed as much. 'I've told you about a dozen times but you don't seem to be listening to me. I haven't seen this man. I don't know him. I've never met him. If my life depended on it, I couldn't identify him. How many ways can I say it? This man is a stranger to me. Why do you keep insisting otherwise?'

The lengthy protest hadn't the slightest impact on the policeman. He seemed totally oblivious to McCabe's discomfort and continued as if nothing had been said. 'Have a look. Perhaps you'll see something that will jolt your memory?' he instructed, pointing towards the body.

Ignoring his comments was enough to annoy McCabe even more. He sighed in frustration. 'There are no memories to jolt, as you call it. The memory bank for this man is empty. You don't get it or you choose not to. Why are you persisting with this moronic and pointless questioning?' The words sounded harsher than he intended and the delivery much louder.

The policeman's body language said it all. He shrugged, almost dismissively. He'd set his mind on a strategy and he was going to follow it to the end. He continued undaunted. 'He's in his sixties, my forensic people tell me,' he added, nodding towards the corpse. 'His hands are rough, a man used to manual labour, we believe. Or at least tough work, wouldn't you say so, Mr. McCabe?'

McCabe, looking resigned to his fate and the determination of the policeman, moved forward again and bent over the body.

The face was worn, lined and weather-beaten, one he would expect from a man who might have spent a lot of time outdoors. Despite his age, he looked trim and fit. But he was dead now and apart from the bruising on his face there was little obvious clue to the reason.

Fischer moved to the side of the corpse and turned its head slightly. A small wound behind the right ear was immediately visible, the unmistakeable hallmark of a bullet, possibly fired by a handgun at close range. He looked at his guest to ensure he'd seen it.

McCabe shook his head and confirmed what he'd already said too many times. 'I don't know him. Why me? Or did you discover the body then select someone at random as a likely suspect, preferably a visiting hack, an innocent vacationer, having a lunchtime cocktail? Or is that illegal too?'

Fischer ignored the comment and returned the head to its previous position.

'It's clear he was murdered. I guess that's what you think, otherwise you wouldn't be taking an interest?' declared McCabe, trying to provoke some feedback.

Again the policeman made no attempt to respond to the remark. 'Would he know you?' he asked, determined to plough on with his questioning.

McCabe was getting even more annoyed now. There didn't seem any way he could make his case. This was not good. 'How the hell should I know?' His voice sounded hoarse now. 'Where is this going?'

Fischer smiled again, this time it contained a hint of humour. He sighed, as if he too was frustrated. For him, this interview wasn't going as planned either. 'I know, you're just a newspaperman on vacation. Is that the story; one of those unexplained coincidences?' He didn't sound as if he believed the account.

McCabe suspected that Fischer came from a long line of cops who didn't believe in coincidences at any time. There had to be a logical explanation for every event, the school of cause and effect. The other possibility was that he was a disciple of the indolent, whose limited curiosity was matched only by a lack of brains and any analytical skill. Somehow, he didn't think the policeman fell into that category. Fischer gave every impression of being a man of tenacity and intelligence.

Fischer pulled the cover back over the body and walked towards the exit at the far end of the room. 'Come with me,' he ordered. 'I hate this place. It always smells of one chemical or another. It gives my sinuses trouble,' he said looking back, nodding at the trolley.

They walked together through a featureless corridor, in serious need of a coat of paint. It didn't smell too inviting either, more musty than anything else. The pungent odour from the lab had managed to penetrate part of it. They stopped at a small door with *Police Chief* written on its frosted glass frontage in bold black letters.

'What's the story then?' asked McCabe impatiently, as he closed the door behind him. 'The dead man; what's his tale? I'll tell you my bit. That's clear enough, at least to me. I was sitting on the balcony outside my hotel bedroom, enjoying the sun, watching the pelicans strutting about in the harbour, caressing a nice long cold cocktail and then, without explanation, I get dragged.....'

Fischer held up his right hand like a policeman on traffic duty. 'Hold it. So, you were dragged this time, were you?' he said, finishing the sentence. 'A little more dramatic than marched, I suppose,' he said with a chuckle. 'Sorry, would you like some iced tea?'

McCabe was caught off balance by the change in direction. 'I guess'.

Chapter 2

St. Augustine, Florida

Fischer looked much too young to be holding down his job, thought McCabe.

His fresh complexion made McCabe feel old, and he was uncomfortable enough already. However, a few minutes in Fischer's company were enough to determine that the policeman was far from naive. He was smart, quick, and wasn't going to be impressed by any Press credentials McCabe would flash at him. The policeman might be only in his late twenties but it was obvious he was used to having his way and wasn't taking any shit from anyone; certainly not from a vacationing hack.

Fischer gestured to a chair in front of his desk. 'Do sit down, Mr. McCabe,' he said politely as he walked to the fridge, poured two glasses of iced tea from a jug, handed one to McCabe and then snuggled himself into a leather seat behind the desk. He spread out a crumpled newspaper cutting in front of him and tried to palm it flat with little success. The more he pressed it, the more it seemed to curl up. Eventually, he held it down, took a mouthful of tea, read the article in silence then leaned back in the chair. 'We didn't find too much to identify him. But we found this in his wallet,' he said as he fingered the stained newsprint.

McCabe leaned forward to catch a glimpse. He could see very little from where he was seated and certainly couldn't read it.

'It's not a very interesting article, in fact there is only part of it here,' said Fischer as he appeared to glance at the article again. 'Yes, we've only got part of it,' he repeated. 'What a pity?' There was more than a hint of sarcasm in his tone. 'It's written by you,' he said quickly, pushing the piece of paper towards McCabe and turning it so he could read it.

'It looks a bit grubby; been in his pocketbook for a while, I guess,' commented McCabe as he inspected the cutting and quickly read the first few paragraphs. It was old, and the policeman was right, it wasn't particularly interesting. There was no headline and not much of the text to tell him what it was about. His by-line had survived.

'You tell me, McCabe. You wrote it,' replied Fischer blandly.

'It doesn't mean anything to me,' said McCabe sounding even more irritated. The cold tea had eased the hoarseness in his voice but his annoyance was still detectable. 'You're not telling me this is the reason you've brought me here; a soiled torn fragment of a newspaper article you found on a dead man?' said McCabe pointing to the cutting. 'What the hell!'

Fischer looked deadpan. He didn't say anything for a moment. It was clear he didn't like the outburst. He began to speak slowly and stressed every word. 'We're not fools here, Mr. McCabe. We may not rub shoulders with the rich and the famous like you people from the Press but we're not stupid either.' He seemed to spit out the last phrase. He stared at the journalist. It was obvious he wasn't giving any quarter. Apparently, there would be no leeway. The policeman was in the driving seat and was confirming that point, emphatically.

McCabe shuffled in his chair. He looked awkward and a little embarrassed. 'I didn't mean to imply .....,' he began. He felt that he may have overstepped a boundary.

Fischer interrupted quickly. 'That we were rednecked cops who didn't know jack shit. You're not the first to make that mistake. We've hosted a few who have voiced that opinion over the years. Our stark accommodation here in the precinct has a miraculous way of altering that view. I'm sure you wouldn't be surprised at that.' The policeman stopped and smiled with satisfaction. He'd made his point again.

Unwittingly, McCabe had crossed a line. He didn't have to say anymore; the apology was written on his face. It wasn't difficult to detect.

Fischer read the expression and nodded in satisfaction. 'Initially, we didn't have any clue to help us positively ID the corpse, but we knew it would come. You see we have this,' he said nodding to the newsprint again.

'Why is that so significant?' asked McCabe, still puzzled by the line of questioning.

Fischer stretched across the table and pointed his right index finger to a barely decipherable scrawl at the bottom of the article.

McCabe squinted but was unable to read it.

'You see, picking you up from your hotel wasn't exactly arbitrary. On close inspection, the handwriting on the bottom of this cutting is quite readable, even though it's not the clearest of scribbles,' Fischer said pulling the cutting close to him. 'Your name is ringed at the top of the article, as you can see, and the writing at the bottom contains the name of the hotel in which you are staying and the number of your room. Now, I'm sure you can work out why you are here? Feel free to have a guess.'

Fischer pulled the cutting back, turned it so he could read it again and looked straight at McCabe, as the phone on his desk rang. He picked it up and instinctively turned away, occasionally looking back at McCabe. If the gesture was meant to intimidate and raise the tension, the strategy worked perfectly. The policeman put the phone slowly onto its cradle and turned back again; in silence for a moment while staring at his guest. 'Why do I get the impression I've come in half way through this?' he said slowly.

McCabe looked at him puzzled. 'You've done what?'

'As if I've walked into a movie half way though,' added Fischer. 'I get the impression, despite your protest, that this isn't a surprise to you.'

'What isn't?'

Fischer nodded towards the door. 'He isn't, the dead guy we've just left,' he replied with a detectable rise in his voice level.

McCabe still looked mystified. 'You've not told me what I'm accused of, how he died and for that matter, what you want from me. You've shown me a newspaper cutting, said who you are, but precious little else. I think I'm entitled to much more. How about some explanation? Or would that be too much to expect? '

The words gushed out in a torrent of complaint. They hadn't been intentional but he'd now established his ground too.
The policeman wrote a few notes onto a pad in front of him then read the contents aloud.
'His name is Harry Meyer. As yet, we don't know who killed him. What we do know is that he is, or was, a neighbour of yours in Washington, a member of your little houseboat community near the DC yacht club on the Potomac River.' McCabe detected a certain edge to his voice, almost a criticism. 'You still claim you don't recognise him? Yet it looks to me as if he was here to see you.'

Fischer opened a drawer, took out a blue folder and flipped it open. He seemed to take an age reading it. He chuckled as he got to the end of the first sheet then quickly turned to the next. 'You would appear to be a bit of a trouble maker, Mr. McCabe.' He turned back to the first page still sniggering. 'How did you manage to get expelled from America? That takes some doing. And I thought this was the land of the free?' he said, still laughing.

'So did I!' responded McCabe. 'On a technical point; I wasn't expelled. My editor recalled me.' He looked genuinely surprised at the policeman's briefing. 'Where did you get that information?' he asked, leaning over the desk trying to read the file.

'As I've told you, down here we're not as backward as some may think. We do have access to an impressive range of data.' He ran his finger down a list on the sheet. 'Getting your address wasn't that difficult either. That's pretty fundamental. And guess what? Your address matched that of our dead friend in the lab,' he said, nodding in the direction of the door again.

McCabe still looked surprised. 'What else is in that file?'

Fischer laughed again. He seemed to be having fun. He looked down and read from the folder. 'A correspondent for a British newspaper, the *London Daily Herald*,' he said as his eyes scanned the sheets in front of him again. 'You're not very popular in the places you've worked, at least among some of the ruling class. Am I right?'

McCabe said nothing. He just stared at the detective, trying to anticipate his next move.

'You definitely are a bit of a troublemaker,' continued Fischer. 'Would you agree with me there?'

'Only if you've got something to hide,' responded McCabe quickly, sounding a little annoyed. 'And what about the dead man?' he added. 'What does your police file say about him?'

Fischer lost his smile. The friendly banter was over. 'Even a death mask can help identify a corpse. With technology, it's all very simple these days.' He forced another smile. 'If a person has a license to drive a car or has been issued with a passport, we can identify him, eventually,' said Fischer with another chuckle.

McCabe didn't say anything for a moment then seemed to gather his thoughts. 'You still haven't told me how he died and where he was found. You didn't tell me anything.'

Fischer tore the note from the pad, rolled it into a ball and threw it into the waste basket at the end of the desk. 'Nor did you Mr. McCabe; nor did you!'

Chapter 3

St. Augustine, Florida

Fischer was standing on the dock waiting for the boat to settle. He could hear the mooring lines strain as they pulled the yacht against the fenders, designed to cushion the effects of any swell. Again and again it rose and dropped. The waves lapped onto the side of the boat and pulled the vessel away from the moorings. The boat bounced uncontrollably in front of him. He waited patiently. He'd plenty of time.

According to the reports he'd received, the boat called *The Georgia*, had drifted ghostlike into St. Augustine harbour in late afternoon two days ago. How it managed without becoming a hazard to shipping was anyone's guess but drift it did, unchallenged by any sailor or floating authority. In true ghostship fashion, there was a sole crew member on board in the form of one dead man whose stiff bruised body gave no clue as to where he had come from, what had happened to him and who was responsible. The only tangible pointers were the markings on the body and a bullet in the back of the skull.

Was this a modern version of the Marie Celeste, the US cargo ship found in the 1800s abandoned with no crew aboard, no clue to their whereabouts or the fate they'd suffered nor at whose hands?

The policeman waited for the boat to settle, quickly ran up the gangway, splayed his feet wide to steady himself on the deck

then made for the cabin. The forensic team had just finished and were packing up, after two hours intensive examination.
Fischer's enquiring look was met with the shake of a head from Dr Glen Barrett, the team leader.

'He was shot here by all accounts, judging by the freshness of the corpse and the blood. We know from the victim's wound that it was an automatic but there were no cartridges found on the deck. We're not sure what that means.'

'Anything else?' fired Fischer, sounding unhappy and impatient. 'Fingerprints?' The question was a little aggressive.

'There are dozens of fingerprints, to be expected; some fairly fresh. But I doubt if they would contribute anything, considering the circumstances.'

Fischer nodded. He hadn't expected much from the forensic inspection, given what had occurred. On its aimless course, the yacht with no sails raised but well secured, had drifted alongside another anchored in the harbour, and had then been boarded by a wave of revellers in full party swing who thought the newcomer was part of the entertainment. After that, it had taken the inebriated mariners more than half an hour to realize that the body lying on the deck was real and very dead. By that time any evidence that might have been preserved, had long been contaminated and was totally worthless. The policeman shook his head in despair.

The forensic team continued packing up their gear. Barrett carried on with his report. 'There are dozens of different old prints. I don't know how many crew this boat needs,' he said looking round him. 'I'm sure you can do the arithmetic. It does have an automatic pilot which appears to have been switched off. So, it was intentionally adrift.' He stopped for a moment. 'One other thing you might be interested in, though.'

Fischer seemed distracted, scouring the boat for anything that might give him some other lead. There were still coloured paper streamers, several empty wine bottles and numerous pieces of clothing littering the deck; remnants of the drunken boarders. These could only cause confusion to their analyses.

'As I said, Chief, one thing you might find interesting,' the forensic repeated. 'This craft has had another life, which perhaps could tell us something about this corpse?'

Fischer didn't catch the implication immediately. 'Can you repeat that?' he said slowly, returning to the conversation.

'*The Georgia* is not the original name of this boat,' said Barrett quite emphatically. 'It's had a previous life, almost certainly. There is plenty of evidence aboard to support that theory.'

'Really?' Fischer now gave his full attention. 'Are you sure?'

The forensic nodded. 'It's not uncommon for a boat to be renamed by a new owner and perhaps used for a different purpose. But somehow I think not in this case.'

'How so?' quizzed Fischer.

'On any boat there is an abundance of indicators showing its original registration, that is, its name and origin. Plaques and labels dotted all over the craft. They are very rarely completely removed or doctored. That's too much bother, unless....' The forensic hesitated. 'And this is only guesswork you understand. I'd hate you to quote me on this.'

Fischer waited for the punchline. He looked impatient again. 'Doctor, please don't do that. If you have something to say, out with it.' He sounded tetchy. He seemed to regret the outburst. His voice now sounded a little softer. 'I need guidance. If you have any thoughts, let's have them. It's all helpful. Let me decide what's relevant. I'll be the judge. That's my job. If you'll forgive the pun, I'm a bit adrift here.' He managed a semblance of a smile.

Barrett looked more relaxed at the concession. He continued. 'They are rarely removed unless the new owner wants to eliminate all traces of the craft's pedigree.'

'All its previous life, as you called it. Why would he do that; perhaps something he didn't want discovered? Like what?'

The scientist nodded. 'Possibly,' he added. 'But more likely for another but obvious reason.'

'What would that be?' asked Fischer, looking a little puzzled. 'You'll have to elaborate on that.'

'If the yacht had been stolen.'

'What?'

The doctor produced his electronic tablet, pressed a few buttons and stared at the screen. He studied it for a moment then read aloud. 'According to the National Insurance Crime Bureau, approximately 6,000 watercraft of different sizes and designs get stolen every year in the USA. Not surprisingly Florida and California rank in the top tier as the favourite spots for theft.

They disappear from ports, marinas, harbours, almost any place where a boat is moored. Some, believe it or not, disappear from driveways on the back of parked trailers. Many will never be seen again, that is, by their original owners.'

'Does it give you much more about this one?' asked Fischer looking at the screen.

The forensic typed in a few more instructions and again inspected the output. 'I'm waiting for a call to confirm something but it would appear the yacht was originally called *The Waverley Princess* and was built about ten miles from here about two years ago. I don't know exactly when and how it changed hands but it was renamed, by the new owner presumably.'

'But you don't know for certain it was stolen?'

'Not yet, but I think it's a good bet.'

Fischer walked slowly along the deck to the gangway. 'Why this boat?' he asked quickly as he turned.

The forensic pulled out a notepad and began to draw a simple sketch of the yacht. He then drew another outline, roughly the same shape but contained in the original contour.

Fischer watched closely as the drawing developed.

'There's an inner skin, a small distance inside the main body of the craft. Because it follows the lines of the boat it's not obvious from inside.'

Fischer looked at the sketch even closer. 'What are you telling me?'

The scientist shrugged. 'It could have been designed that way, or installed by the new owner?'

'For what purpose?' pressed Fischer.

'Now there's a question.'

'How about an answer?' insisted Fischer, sounding impatient again.

'The boat looked as if it could have been designed to carry concealed cargo. It has numerous cubbyholes in which to secrete merchandise or people; intriguing don't you think; installed, perhaps, by the new owner. There again, it may be perfectly innocent.'

Fischer frowned. He wasn't keen on the uncertainty of the answer. 'Thanks. That about covers every eventuality.'

'He may have had someone steal it for him,' the forensic added, as he finished packing his gear into a small leather case. 'They usually steal to order.'

'Who are they?'

'Some are professional maritime thieves who then give the boat a facelift, a name change then sell it on. Sometimes equally talented mariners sell their skills to those who've had their boats stolen.'

'To do what?' fired Fischer.

'To reclaim them, of course!'

'You mean steal them back?'

The scientist smiled. 'I think they call it reclaim.'

Fischer thought for a moment. 'The guy we found on the deck, the dead man; where does he fit into your theory? Is that what he was here for?'

The forensic zipped up his bag, walked towards the gangway shaking his head slowly. 'I'm not going to get drawn into that, Chief; not my province. You're the Police Chief; my job is forensic science. I'm leaving the detection to you.' He got to the edge of the boat and stopped. 'Almost forgot,' he said pulling out a small brown envelope and handing it to Fischer. 'The yacht was fairly clean but this was stuck at the bottom of one of the dustbins.'

The policeman opened the envelope, had a quick look then sniffed the content. He pulled his head back quickly. It smelled rancid.

'It's a cigarette butt of some description,' said the forensic. 'It appears a little unusual but that might be the salt water.'

'It smells putrid; any guesses?'

The forensic smiled then laughed a little. 'You're giving me a lot of leeway today, Chief.'

Fischer said nothing for a moment. 'Is that a nautical term?' He even forced a smile.

'It's definitely foreign, I'd say. I'll let you know soonest.'

'No guesses, then,' said Fischer, pushing him.

The forensic nodded. 'OK, have it your way. I'll know more after I've had a chance to examine the relevant bits but at a guess, I'd say Eastern European, perhaps Russian.'

Chapter 4

St. Augustine, Florida

About three hundred yards from *The Georgia* was a good vantage point to watch the activity in the harbour. It didn't need an ace investigative journalist to determine that this boat was the focus of local police activity. Uniforms and patrol cars were in evidence all along the quayside, near the gangway to the yacht. McCabe watched the excitement intently.

Ten minutes earlier, from the comfort of an upstairs lounge in a bar overlooking the harbour, as he savoured one of his favourite Tequila-based cocktails, he'd watched as Fischer inspected the mooring then boarded the yacht. The Police Chief hadn't looked any more relaxed than he'd done the previous day, but was in deep discussion with one of his team.

McCabe had finished his drink and made for the quayside. He couldn't be privy to what the police had discovered, but there were other sources. It was a good guess that the dead man had been found on the boat or close to it. The police activity would seem to suggest that. For some reason, Fischer had chosen not to share those details with him. Also, whatever crew had been on board hadn't been around to identify the dead man, otherwise Fischer wouldn't have called on him. That much he'd been able to deduce. He didn't know anything for sure but it was as good a conclusion as any. He had to start somewhere.

So, who might know more? Logically, bringing a boat into harbour invites a string of regulations. There is always the tedium of bureaucracy and the paperwork. In this case it could be a godsend. Sailing a yacht into a US harbour is not like parking a car. Even a drifting boat might have to observe certain proprieties, if not a myriad of rules. McCabe's next stop was obvious, the official looking building, prominently positioned on the quayside with an impressive US Department of Homeland Security seal on the wall.

There didn't seem to be a lot of activity inside.

'No one in there; not this time of day,' said a voice from behind him, as he tried to open the office door. He turned slowly to locate the source, seated on a bench by the quay about twenty feet away, smoking the stub of a fat cigar.

'Any idea when someone might be back?' asked McCabe, moving away from the door towards the smoker.

'I don't know. I'm just sitting here having a smoke. Not too many places a man can do that these days,' he said in a rather husky voice with a laugh. He looked in his late sixties, and a little unkempt or casually dressed, depending on how charitable the description.

'Do you live on the water?' asked McCabe. It was a fair introduction, he thought. Whatever the answer, it should start some conversation. 'My name is Mike McCabe.'

The cigar smiled back. He made no introduction but it got some reaction.

Maybe McCabe had fired a lucky shot.

'Live on the water?' repeated the old man. 'Is there any other way?' It was a statement, not a question. 'It's in our blood, you know,' he continued. 'It's where we all came from.' He seemed to drift into some philosophical mist for a moment.

McCabe was barely listening, just catching the odd phrase, enough to keep up. He had thought of telling him about his rented houseboat in Washington and the one he owned in London, but he guessed it might sound a little trite.

'I live on a little sailboat at the other end of the harbour,' the old man added.

'You live there permanently?' asked McCabe, as he reached the bench.

The old man stood up, stretched himself and inhaled another mouthful from his smouldering cigar. The tip glowed bright red. He blew out the result quickly and then watched as the smoke drift away. 'Officially, no; the bureaucrats don't like that,' he said, nodding towards the office. 'I was born not far from here but I take my little boat up and down the Florida coast. I've retired now.'

'From what?' persisted McCabe.

'You do ask a lot of questions,' he said, finishing the cigar and flipping the remains into the water.

'Sorry, occupational hazard. I'm a journalist. I'm writing a story about this area.' It wasn't a total lie. He felt comfortable with the statement.

'I'm Charlie Banks,' said the old man, as he pulled out another cigar and lit it. 'I've done a bit of everything; fishing, boatbuilding, tour guide; all the above. Where are you from? You don't look or sound from these parts. Are you Australian?' McCabe laughed. 'No, British'. Again, he was tempted to tell him about his houseboats but he guessed it would sound even more ridiculous now. 'I was interested in that,' he said pointing towards *The Georgia.*

The old man followed the line of McCabe's pointed finger. He nodded and muttered something to himself quietly. 'You mean the *Princess*?'

'No,' replied McCabe immediately. 'The yacht at the end of the quay, where I'm pointing; it's called *The Georgia.*'

'Is that a fact,' said the old man, shaking his head. He said nothing for a moment as he stared in the direction of the yacht. 'It wasn't when she left here a few years ago. I knew the man who built her; a fine piece of workmanship she is too. I'd know her anywhere. She was called the *Waverley Princess* then. A damn fine craft and, if you knew how to sail her, damn fast too. She could beat anything under sail in these waters.'

'Are you sure?' asked McCabe cautiously. He tried not to sound unconvinced.

'Boats that have been made to order have their own personality. She's as sleek as anything built in these parts,' he added. 'As sleek as anything built in these parts,' he repeated. 'Men and boys dream of sailing round the world in a boat like that,' he said, locked into his philosophical trance again.

'Personality?' repeated McCabe, sounding cynical.

Banks shook his head. 'You're definitely not from around here? You wouldn't ask that question otherwise.' He nodded as if agreeing with his own statement. 'Definitely, not from around here,' he added quickly.

McCabe couldn't resist the temptation any more. He felt compelled to defend his credentials. 'I live on the water too; a houseboat in DC and I have one in London.' It still sounded trite.

The old man smiled. 'Well you know what I mean then. The ones that are manufactured are not those I'm talking about. The *Princess* was crafted, not forged out of plastic.'

'Who owned it?'

Banks drew heavily on his new cigar. 'I'll tell you one thing. It was built for some purpose other than fishing. I'm sure of that.'

Chapter 5

St. Augustine, Florida

Darlene Shannon, member of the Coastal Intelligence Unit, examined the data sent from headquarters in Washington, DC, displayed on her tablet. She'd sought confirmation of the name of a yacht, now the centre of police enquiries in St. Augustine harbour, and any details of the incident which so occupied the authorities buzzing around the harbour.

Her interest in this particular vessel was well established. Over several months she and her team had tracked the erratic and seemingly mysterious course of the craft, now called *The Georgia*, as it sailed up the Florida coast and back.

She pressed a few more keys on her phone. Different pieces of software analysed the information and displayed the results on screen. The data culled from every time the vessel legitimately registered in a port was logged. It couldn't account for visits where registration was unnecessary or when *The Georgia* was anchored offshore. One correlation and permutation after another had been tried by the statisticians in DC. There were gaps in the basic information, vital in establishing a pattern. Now that Meyer was dead, they might never get the last bits of the jigsaw that had also become fuzzy. Additionally, *The Georgia* was in dock, under armed guard, designated a crime scene and in quarantine.

She pulled on her jacket, and checked the full-length mirror to ensure there was no bulge from her automatic, housed in a small holster on her waist. Her plans had been altered dramatically in the past twenty-four hours. The man she'd been trailing for the last several weeks was now splayed on a police mortuary slab with a bullet in the back of his skull. She didn't have an explanation why it had all gone wrong. Her superiors wanted one and soon. She didn't have one.

But that was part of the job in this arm of the US Coast Guard. She felt the unit to be an unsung hero of the intelligence community. There were thousands of miles of coast and hundreds of ports and harbours to be protected in a century where people-smuggling, drugs and terrorism were commonplace. The US beaches were as vulnerable as any national border. She didn't take her job lightly.

Also for her, the job was results driven. Failure couldn't be countenanced; not in her world. She knew she was considered, by some, to be pushy and ambitious. It mattered little their opinion. She loved the service and felt confident that she held her own against some of the more experienced agents, particularly the men with distinguished military careers. She knew there were tensions among colleagues, provoked by jealousies and rivalries. There were also those, endemic in every security agency, as they plied for recognition. But that wasn't a road she was going down. There were enough issues to deal with without interagency rivalry. Chasing political shadows and irrelevancies sapped the energy. She had to remain focused. That was her primary challenge.

Her route had been via university. She was smart and she knew it. What's more, anyone who'd worked with her knew that too. It was a burden as well as a blessing, which bred jealousy above loyalty. However, she'd survived. After the initial jousting and intellectual sparring when she'd first joined the service, things settled down. The contest hadn't abated though, and she reminded herself of it frequently. Whether it would have been the same had she been a man, she would never know. She didn't care. She'd clipped a few wings. Few of the roosters in this particular barnyard crowed overtly now but the Neanderthal male persona hadn't quite disappeared. She suspected it would have a permanent presence.

She typed a few more instructions into the tablet. A secure email contained the attachment she'd requested. The screen filled with article after article; the biography of the man the police had taken from his hotel and questioned at their headquarters. Its content was a surprise. It painted a picture of a dedicated, if stubborn and tenacious British journalist. After reading the screeds, she wasn't sure if trouble followed him or he was attracted to it. Whatever, it appeared to be part of his world.

The story of Mike McCabe was amusing in parts. Some of his activities appeared subtle, others less so, as he blundered albeit courageously into one dangerous predicament after another. His newspaper, the *London Daily Herald*, had no shortage of praise for its newshound but unquestionably it was biased. Other authors in the profile collection had expressed as many reservations as they gave accolades. None challenged his dedication, ethics and skill but others considered him an idealist, if not a naive boy scout.

She scanned the screen again. There was plenty of detail but it didn't give her the answers for which she'd been searching. Did McCabe know what had happened on the boat? Why was Meyer killed? Did this journalist, who was supposedly on vacation, know any more than she did? Why did the police interview him and even insist that he identify the victim? But the paramount question was obvious. What was he doing in St. Augustine? The answer might be as complex as the man himself. One blatant truth was clear from his file. Mike McCabe had never taken a vacation in his life.

The Georgia still bounced about as McCabe watched from his hotel balcony, supping another cocktail. There were two uniformed police with rifles on either side of the boat's gangway now. He wasn't going to be able to get on board without approval from Fischer or his merry men. And that wasn't likely.

He didn't think the police knew any more about the killing than they had done earlier. Perhaps Meyer had been shot accidently? That wasn't probable. He obviously didn't do it to himself, although there would appear to be no evidence of another person on board. However, it was obvious from Meyer's cutting and the scrawl on it, who the police thought he'd come to see. Chief Fischer was no fool.

The conversation with the old man on the quayside had given McCabe some lines of enquiry but he'd yet to determine in what direction. The veteran mariner seemed genuine, although a little fanciful. To believe him would require quite a leap of faith.

McCabe's original plans were now in tatters. He was supposed to be in town to write a feature on the oldest town in the USA, originally colonised by the Spanish and eventually annexed into the new America. It was a good subject and the editorial bosses back in London seemed happy. He'd clock up a few bonus points with the idea. But now there had been a dramatic change of plan triggered by the death of Meyer, the man whose lifeless body now adorned the police forensic lab.

He hadn't told Fischer the entire truth, although strictly speaking he hadn't lied either. He'd had a phone call from Harry Meyer, out of the blue, a few days earlier. They had planned to meet up, in obviously different circumstances. But the man was a total stranger. It was news that they had been neighbours in Washington. That fact, not surprisingly, made the police uneasy. McCabe claiming he didn't know him made them even more suspicious.

To be fair, it wasn't the first time that someone, whom he'd never heard of, had contacted him with what they thought was *a story*. Too many times the tale was inaccurate or wasn't quite as dramatic as the teller suggested. Some were good but had already been published with a few questionable elements and dimensions added in the retelling. Most were a waste of time. He'd assumed the same was true in this case but only agreed because he had already planned to be in St. Augustine to do the feature.

Now the picture was much more complex.

'They're authorised pirates,' the old man on the quayside had claimed. 'You want a boat. Like car thieves, they steal to order. They don't have wooden legs, parrots and patches on their eyes these days. Some are thieves, some work for insurance companies, some even work for the government. They sail under pirates' articles,' he'd added, laughing all the while. 'But the facts are the same. They steal, repossess, relocate, however you like to describe it. I reckon that boat was stolen to order.'

No amount of staring from the hotel balcony at *The Georgia* was going to give McCabe any answers. He knew that much. Meyer was dead, for whatever reason. Did this poor man have a story of any interest to tell or was his death one of those tragic coincidences? And the boat; did that play any part in his tale? He had no idea what the dead man was about to tell, if anything. It could be a waste of time, chasing shadows while his newspaper back in London waited for his article. But that was the game he was in; pursuing the slightest hint of a story, whatever the risks. For the moment, Meyer's story interested him much more than a profile about this particular piece of Floridian paradise.

He finished the cocktail and was in his car within five minutes. He glanced at the notes he'd made after the conversation with the old man on the quayside. He'd given him a name. The address was easy to find. He checked his map then started the car. He'd be there in half an hour.

Chapter 6

St. Augustine, Florida

Jim Ryan's boatyard wasn't difficult to find, although McCabe did have to resort to GPS. He pulled up beside the double-fronted white wooden gate at the entrance. He parked then wandered through the boatyard. About three yachts were mounted in dry docks. Two looked as if they were getting a major repaint and a facelift. The third was a new-build in the final stages of construction.

Above the office was a sign in large black letters on a white background. It read: *From a long line of Irish smugglers.*

McCabe read the sign more than once. 'Really,' he said, trying to disguise his cynicism.

'You don't believe it, do you?' said the man behind him with a laugh. Jim Ryan paused for a moment and chuckled again. 'Neither do I but it's an interesting family myth; something to tell the customers.'

To say Ryan had a ruddy complexion was an understatement. His skin looked as if it had been stretched in the sun for decades, pickled in sea salt to give it a taut and leathered look with a sprinkling of grey in his otherwise black hair. His teeth had fallen victim to neglect, a condition enhanced by either chewing or smoking the dreaded weed. But he was a cheery soul, smiled a lot and was far from being self-conscious of his gaping grin.

'Is that what you told the buyer of *The Georgia*?' asked McCabe.

'So that's why you're here?'

'You're the naval architect?'

Ryan's laugh was loud and mocking. 'A bit pretentious that description; I design and build boats, plain and simple. You're here about the yacht that drifted into the harbour a day or so ago with a corpse on board?' He paused again. 'Sad, very sad.'

'Why do you say that? Did you know the man who was found?'

'I'm talking about the boat. But not being a sailor, you wouldn't know anything about that would you?'

'It's not the first time I've heard that line since I've been here.'

'Seafaring people have a different view of life,' replied Ryan still chuckling.

'Tall stories to go with tall ships?' replied McCabe quickly. The words sounded harsh and the sentiment bitter. Neither was what he intended. 'I'm sorry, I didn't mean.....'

Ryan interrupted quickly shaking his head. 'Whether you believe that or not, it's not important.' He stopped and studied McCabe for a moment. 'You're the journalist who's been asking questions in the harbour about the yacht?'

'How did you know that?' asked McCabe quickly.

Ryan laughed loudly showing his few remaining teeth. 'News travels fast in a boating community.'

'You're right. I'm Mike McCabe, pleased to meet you,' he said, extending his right hand for a handshake.

'It's been altered,' replied Ryan taking his hand and shaking it with a firm grip.

'Altered?' echoed McCabe.

'She wasn't called *The Georgia* then. She was registered the *Waverley Princess*. She's different from the boat that left this yard.'

'How?'

'If you have the right eye, you can tell these things.'

'How?' McCabe felt he was badgering the builder. He was.

'The way it moves through the water, its trim. Loading and passenger distribution can alter trim too. That yacht has been doctored,' insisted Ryan.

'To do what?'

'I haven't inspected it but I could guess.' The laughter had gone out of his voice. It was obvious he considered any alteration to be an abomination. His craftsmanship had been compromised. He wasn't pleased.

'Be my guest, speculate,' encouraged McCabe. 'I can tell you took pride in the original.'

Ryan's smile returned. 'Yes,' he said sounding almost boastful. 'That yacht would take on any boat that ever left these waters. She was designed to be fast.'

'I'm told new owners alter boats as a matter of course,' said McCabe repeating what the old man had told him. It made him sound knowledgeable.

Ryan looked at him strangely. He seemed to know that the knowledge was second hand. 'Yes, altered to carry particular cargo, perhaps concealed.'

McCabe cynical look returned. 'How can you tell that?'

Ryan screwed up his face and shook his head. 'I can't but there was plenty more cupboards and storage space. So rumour has it.'

McCabe was still not convinced by the rhetoric but was trying to sound open-minded. It was proving difficult. 'Not being a sailor, I guess I can't quite grasp that,' he said apologetically. He tried to sound credible.

Ryan didn't buy it. He looked at McCabe and shook his head. 'An unbeliever,' he added as he burst out laughing again. 'I'm guessing based on what they usually do with stolen boats.'

'They sell them for money, presumably?' prompted McCabe.

The boat builder was serious again. 'Some do, yes. But a new registration can sometimes be difficult, if you want to convince a legitimate buyer.'

McCabe's voice changed its tone. He was now getting persuaded. 'You mean the people who buy them are crooks too?'

The toothless grin appeared again. 'Or stole it to keep for themselves. There are dozens of them sailing round the world, a flotilla of stolen yachts, transporting every illegal cargo known to man and a few they have yet to discover. Criminal traffic carried by thieves, drug-runners and peddlers of all sorts of human traffic. Who knows for what purpose?'

'Did you tell the police?'

Ryan didn't need to reply. He gave a look in response which said it all. Eventually he spoke. 'I'm not likely to do that, am I?' he added. 'We're in coastal waters. There's been smuggling here since this was a Spanish colony.'

McCabe recalled his conversation with the old man in the harbour about the people who stole yachts or repossessed them for their legitimate owners. He'd said, quite emphatically, *Some are thieves, some work for insurance companies, some even work for the government.* 'What about the guy they found dead on the yacht?' he asked quickly, changing the subject.

Ryan shrugged his shoulders. 'Perhaps he stole it in the first place. Maybe things went wrong for him.' He didn't seem overly concerned about the dead man. He didn't seem concerned about him at all. 'What do you want from me, sympathy? I've no love for thieves. Apparently, he lived in Washington. His name was Harry Meyer.'

McCabe looked surprised. 'You're well informed.'

Ryan's grin reappeared. 'I told you news travels fast in a boating community. I also hear you knew him.'

McCabe looked annoyed, as he shook his head in obvious denial. 'That's where your bush telegraph has failed you, Mr. Ryan. Apparently he was a neighbour of mine. I didn't know him.' He thought he might tell him about the houseboat and its community. But somehow now it would have sounded even more trivial than before.

He could understand Ryan's point but there was no compromise; no middle ground. 'Suppose he was trying to reclaim the boat, wouldn't that make a difference?'

'In the way I thought about him?' he asked with his voice rising. 'You don't get it McCabe. I don't care. The boat is my only concern.' He stopped talking, as if he was going to qualify what he'd said. But it was soon evident he'd no regrets. 'They shouldn't have messed about with her; she was a great boat. It's been used for different purposes for which I designed her.'

'The guy who commissioned her; what was he going to use her for?'

'She was designed for fishing but to be fast. The original owner went bust and never took possession of the boat. So I sold it to someone else,' he said looking at his watch. 'That reminds me. The new owner needs some paperwork from me.'

'What about him? Would he have hired Meyer to reclaim his boat?'

Ryan shook his head. 'All I know is that he's going to court to reclaim the boat. Why don't you ask him yourself? I'm sure he'd be happy to speak to you.'

Chapter 7

St. Augustine, Florida

McCabe cautiously negotiated the driveway of an address, given by Ryan, about ten miles outside of the town. He sat in the car mystified. If he hadn't known better, he would have sworn that he had just arrived at the White House in Washington. It was slightly smaller but identical in every detail. What did that say about the man he was about to interview; pretentious, vain, ambitious? He would soon find out.

Randolph Warren was a local property developer and entrepreneur. Apparently, nothing was immune from his investment lust; small shopping malls, mobile-home parks, racquet-ball courts and low-cost housing developments.

McCabe inspected the text of his tablet. It said Warren was a successful self-made man, if making money was a measure. Originally from New York, he'd visited Florida on vacation, ten years before, one of the many 'snow birds' who'd arrived in that warm sunny spring. He'd never left, smitten by the Florida bug. He appeared to love his lifestyle and the opportunities it gave him to flaunt his wealth. The web and the local newspapers were full of his exploits, most of them obvious, if not crass, exercises in self-publicity.

McCabe shouldered the car door open and crunched his way up the gravel path. Not surprisingly, the door bell was gold coloured and inordinately loud. Somehow, it seemed in keeping. He let out a long sigh as the bell rang.

Again, not surprisingly, the door was answered by a manservant in a black coat-tailed jacket and white gloves. It all added to the image he already had of the local businessman. He was shown into the lounge and waited for what seemed several minutes before his host appeared with a predictably loud greeting.

'You said on the phone that you're here to talk about *The Georgia*?' He didn't wait for an answer. 'Can I get you something to drink?'

'Scotch with a little ice, would be nice,' answered McCabe quietly, taken aback by the politeness.

Warren smiled, as he poured the drink. 'I heard you were fond of a good whisky. You'll find this to your taste, I'm sure,' he said handing over the glass. 'I'll join you, and please do sit down,' he added pointing to the chairs in the centre of the sitting room.

McCabe sipped the drink cautiously. His host was right; the whisky was excellent. He studied Warren's face. He could have been Mexican, Cuban, Spanish-American or something in between. In the great melting pot of Florida, it was difficult to determine which one.

Warren was tanned, stocky with a face that was lined and eyes that appeared unforgiving. It wasn't difficult to imagine him on the winning side of any negotiations. He had rings on almost every finger and when he wasn't looking at them he was stroking his black, short hair. McCabe felt uneasy. 'You seem remarkably well informed,' said McCabe. 'Even down to my drinking preferences.'

'The boating fraternity is close-knit. News travels.'

'So you know why I'm here?'

Warren smiled and nodded. 'Of course; as I said, news travels. You're a journalist. Do I need to know any more?'

One serious impediment to any interview was a question being answered by a question. McCabe hoped it wasn't going to be one of those. 'I'm told you're the original owner of the *Waverley Princess* or *The Georgia*, as she is now,' said McCabe with no preamble.

'Not quite,' Warren replied quickly. 'The original owner went bust, couldn't pay for it,' he added with no sympathy in his voice. 'I bought it from the builder,' he added as he pulled out a pair of clippers and cut the end from a large cigar. He looked admiringly at the cigar as he twirled it between the fingers of his right hand. 'I don't know what all the fuss is about. They've been available in the streets here for years.'

McCabe looked puzzled. He'd lost the thread of the conversation. He'd been sidetracked.

'The cigars,' added Warren with a laugh. 'They even have billboards on the high street; *Genuine Cuban Cigars* they claim. They've been smuggling here since the place was a Spanish colony.'

McCabe smiled. 'I've heard that said.' He tried not to sound cynical as he watched Warren light his cigar and draw heavily on it. 'Are they the same?' he asked quickly, aware of the diversion, and nudging the conversation back on track. 'The two yachts, I mean; are you sure they're the same?'

'No doubt; I've been all over her,' said Warren caressing his cigar again. 'I needed a court order to do it and couldn't go near the parts sectioned off by the police, but it's her alright. You can change the name of a yacht but there's something unique about every vessel, certainly the ones that have been crafted as she has been.'

'So I've heard,' responded McCabe, again sounding unconvinced.

'Glad to have her back. Do you know that hundreds of boats are stolen every year by thieves and the owners never see them again? This one was stolen a year ago from this very port.'

McCabe remained focused. 'I've also been told that the same people are hired by owners to highjack or reclaim their own vessels.'

'Is that so?' replied Warren, claiming ignorance. 'Look Mr. McCabe, I don't know what your interest is here. Perhaps if you tell me, I can help?'

As McCabe expected, Warren's attention span was very limited. McCabe was groping in the dark, trying to get a lead on the yacht, on Meyer and why they'd drifted together into the local harbour. There was a slight chance the owner of the boat might know but it was a long shot. He had to go through the motions.

'Do you think the dead man stole the boat from you?'

'How should I know?' snapped Warren.

McCabe sensed the tension. The atmosphere had turned a little sour.

'Why don't you come straight out with it and ask me if I hired this guy to get my boat back?'

McCabe didn't like this guy. He didn't seem to have any redeeming features. 'OK; did you?'

'I don't employ people to break the law. I'm a business man.'

'Of course you don't,' replied McCabe. He was hoping the reply sounded unconvincing. It was meant to. 'But I have to ask the question.' It was an apology of sorts.

Warren was still looking disturbed. Clearly, he didn't like the direction of the conversation. 'There's going to come a time fairly soon when this discussion has to stop,' he said bluntly. The mood definitely had gone sour.

'It was getting interesting too,' replied McCabe quickly, hoping to cater to his host's vanity. 'I thought you might enjoy a challenging conversation?'

Warren didn't respond. His facial expression painted the picture. He looked annoyed. 'What are you after, Mr.McCabe? I'm at a loss to imagine how I can help you?'

McCabe made an attempt at rescue. 'I'm doing a story on the town. A drifting unmanned yacht with a dead man on board is as good an intro to a feature than any I can imagine. What do you think?'

Warren seemed to relax a little at the answer.

But he wasn't here for small talk. He had to keep pushing. 'Can I ask you if you found what you were looking for?' said McCabe, trying to prevent the question sounding intrusive.

'What do you mean?' snapped Warren.

McCabe thought for a moment about his answer. He didn't want this fox to get startled and run for cover. To hell with the caution, he thought. 'You knew the boat was yours just by looking at her. You've already told me as much. So, what were you looking for?'

'To see if she was intact and not damaged. Is that so strange?'

It was a perfectly logical answer, thought McCabe. But there was something else; he was sure. Every instinct told him that Warren was holding something back. But he'd no idea what. He'd have one last salvo. 'Was there something you needed to check before anyone else got to her?'

Warren stood up slowly. 'It was nice to meet you Mr. McCabe. Good luck on your article,' he said as he pressed a small button on one side of the drinks cabinet.

In an instant, the manservant, who had opened the front door, appeared.

'My guest is leaving,' said Warren, almost clinically. 'Please show him out.'

Things hadn't gone as planned. He didn't need to be an ace reporter to reach that conclusion. But he was annoyed. Perhaps a less obvious approach would have produced a better result. Had he touched a nerve with his questions? Was there something of value on *The Georgia* when she'd been stolen or perhaps Warren expected a cargo to be aboard when the yacht drifted into St. Augustine? The answers might give him a clue to why Meyer was on board the yacht and why he was murdered. Whatever it was, it was important to Warren and he wasn't disclosing what it was, particularly to an inquisitive journalist.

Walking back to his car, McCabe felt that while his questioning might have lacked a little finesse, he doubted if any answers from Warren would have explained the circumstances surrounding the death of Harry Meyer. The interview with him had turned into farce.

Perhaps the billionaire was just a control freak and there was nothing to be had from him? His ego demanded he give a different impression. It was probable he didn't know anything more than anyone else. That's what galled the billionaire the most.

It may have been a dead end after all; big deal!

McCabe started up the car and caught a glimpse of a small blue Ford leaving a parking bay. He thought a similar one had followed him the previous day when he'd gone to the boatyard. Now, it had turned up again. There was no shortage of blue Fords in Florida but he was certain it was the same one. It told him someone was taking an interest in him, or, more importantly, in the story he was pursuing. There was nothing like a probing question or two to create a few waves.

Chapter 8

Washington, DC

The tyres from the Delta flight screeched and smoked as they hit the runway at National Airport in Washington, DC. McCabe was always amazed, if not a little nervous, when landing at this particular airport. A stone's throw from the centre of the capital, it was so close that from the air traffic control tower almost every historic landmark of the city was visible. It was a startling landing but more than a little traumatic.

A quick cab ride and he was back on his houseboat, moored near the DC Yacht Club on the Potomac estuary. It was early afternoon. He poured himself his first beer of the day. After all, he had been up since seven. It was as good a justification as any.

On deck he could quite clearly see the boat which belonged to Harry Meyer. He had seen the neighbour at a distance several times but had never spoken to him. Even in this close-knit maritime community, where the members were proud of looking out for each other, he'd never exchanged a single greeting. Also, he doubted if he could have recognised him in any other context outside the marina. The first time he'd met the man, if that was the description, was when a Florida cop unveiled his corpse.

He walked across the deck several times wondering when would be a good time to do what he'd come back to DC to do? What he was contemplating wasn't his bag but he couldn't see any other way forward. He sat at the front of the boat and tried to get his thoughts in order.

That was an easy task; there wasn't much to sort out. It was a simple list. To determine its significance was a different challenge.

Meyer, a neighbour whom he didn't know, had died violently on board a stolen yacht which had drifted, unmanned, into the waters near St. Augustine on the east-Florida coast. The bruising on the corpse and a bullet lodged in the back of its brain didn't tell much. There was no identification on him, no clue as to why he was there and no hint to what had provoked his attack. All he had on him was a flimsy cutting from a newspaper with its by-line ringed, and McCabe's hotel and room number scribbled on its torn bottom edge. On the basis of that evidence, McCabe had been hauled in by the police to identify a man he'd never met.

The only sensible strategy was to go back to the source. The Florida Police Chief couldn't do anything outside his patch. But McCabe could, or at least he intended to try. He looked at his watch. In about four hours it would be dark, the shoppers who came to the fish market a few blocks away would have gone, the stallholders would have packed up their wares, the delivery vans would be sorting out the next day's orders; perfect cover for what he needed to do. Before he did that, he had to do the basics; find out about the man whose death had triggered a whole wave of activity in Florida and now in DC.

He logged into a couple of databases he used when checking on archived cuttings and published biographies. He had little difficulty in retrieving some superficial data. The veteran, dedicated and professional navy man had kept his life well concealed. As a fellow member of the DC nautical community, he was the living cliché; the one who kept himself to himself. But the published biography, not unexpectedly, was limited. It was a PR product. Everyone had incidents that lurked in the shadows of one's CV but there was nothing visible. Harry Meyer was a superhero and a patriot. It begged the obvious questions. What was he doing aboard a stolen yacht and what had he done to merit a slug in the back of his head?

McCabe walked carefully along the pontoon. The sun had gone down and the only lights were those on the exteriors of the houseboats in the marina, bobbing up and down in the swell, and floodlights at either end of the pontoon. An occasional headlight from a car driving through the trees on the other riverbank invaded the darkness like a searchlight but not enough to break his cover. He stopped and listened. The only sound was the lapping of the water on the sides of the boats and the noise as they bumped into their rubber tyres, buffering their hulls from the pontoon. Meyer's boat was in the shadows, another layer to the camouflage he prayed would keep his visit secret. He was also hoping the crowbar beneath his coat wouldn't betray his purpose. It would be difficult to explain.

He had a quick check for anyone who may have appeared on the quayside or on the adjacent boats before he raced forward. He reached the gangway and was on deck in seconds. He moved quickly to the entrance of the cabin. The door was locked, as expected. He listened again for the slightest sound. He hesitated as he stuck the crowbar behind the lock. This wasn't what he did; why was he doing this? He felt nervous and unsure of the plan. But Meyer was dead and wouldn't be reporting any break in. Nevertheless, it was still a felony. He stepped back, pushed the metal rod as far forward and as hard as he could. He heard the lock crack, the door splinter and the noise echo across the water. He was surprised at the loudness and stood quite still, almost expecting some reaction; a voice raising an alarm, a dog barking, a flashlight shining in his direction. Nothing! A long sigh eased out of him. He felt it could be heard all along the quayside but again there was no reaction. He was getting more nervous by the second. There was still only silence. He carefully pulled the door of the cabin open, slipped quietly inside and felt his way down the dark stairwell into the lounge. It took only a few more seconds to close the curtains and put on the lights. He sat down on the sofa, slightly breathless and still nervous. He would have loved a very large Black Label; no such luck. His heart was pounding, so hard he didn't move for a minute. Slowly, he got to his feet.

He wasn't certain about the rest of the plan. Whatever he decided to do, it had to be done quickly. Amateur though he was, he knew that much. The more he dallied, the more dangerous, and the greater the likelihood of discovery. By whom, he wasn't sure but he wasn't going to test the theory. Explaining this little episode, to anyone except the most gullible, would have rigorously tested even his imaginative storytelling skills.

He looked round the cabin to get his bearings. There didn't seem to be anything in its correct place. It was a picture of chaos, mayhem and confusion. It was unlikely to be Meyer's doing. Someone had already been in the cabin, ransacking any container, drawer or cupboard, looking for something. Even the flower vases had been turned upside down and their contents dumped recklessly on the carpet. There was no order to this looting, if ever there was such a thing. It was a mess and whoever was responsible was frantic. It was easy to visualise the violence of the search as the level of frustration rose, for document after document had been carelessly discarded, adding to the chaos. Whoever had sacked the lounge was looking for something and in a hurry. It was obvious too that if the intruders had found what they were looking for, it clearly hadn't surfaced until the end. Of course, there was every chance they hadn't found anything.

In the next ten minutes, McCabe followed suit. He rustled through every drawer and cupboard on the houseboat, including the contents tipped onto the carpet. Even the galley got similar treatment. He had no idea what he was looking for but perhaps there was something that would tell him why this man had died a thousand or so miles from his home with a bullet in his skull, floating towards the Florida coast, alone, aboard a stolen yacht.

But there were still some additional questions. Harry Meyer, a supposed quiet-living neighbour, had attracted the attention of the criminal class on at least two occasions. In the first he'd been beaten and murdered and in the second what was left of his dignity had been violated in this invasion of his personal space. It was clear now that the quiet man who lived in this comfortable nautical urban community had another life, one which was not as it appeared to be to his neighbours and one that had made him a target for murder.

However, the houseboat search hadn't entirely been a waste of time. Clearly, Meyer had something which was of value, so desirable in fact that he may have paid with his life when protecting it. But breaking into his houseboat hadn't exposed any secrets. The results of McCabe's rummaging added nothing to his bank of knowledge. He could speculate all night long but it would get him nowhere. There was no scrap of paper containing the slightest reference to his activities aboard *The Georgia*. Curiously, there was no evidence of his previous life as a navy veteran either. Such absence told him something. His other lives didn't exist. There was no evidence of any life outside the houseboat; no photographs, no letters, no postcards, no reminder notes pinned to the galley notice board or the computer, in fact, no computer. There was no clue to what went on outside this floating refuge; no evidence of who occupied it or what he did inside or out. Even the fridge told him nothing; orange juice, milk, eggs and coffee was all that could be seen.

No magnets stuck to the fridge door to remind him of what to buy or as mementos from vacations; nothing.

McCabe switched off the lights and carefully opened the curtains. There was still no one to be seen; the quayside and the pontoon were empty. In the dark he felt his way to the top of the stairwell. It was only when he reached the top that he saw the small red light flashing in the far corner of the room. He carefully retraced his steps then manoeuvred his way in the dark towards it, bumping into several pieces of furniture on the way. The red light disappeared as he picked up the telephone from its cradle and pressed the message button. A young man's voice pierced the silence.

'This is Gary from Maritime Excursions. Regarding your enquiries about the *Orient Atlantic*; give me a call back. Thanks.

The message was timed two days earlier.

Chapter 9

Washington, DC

The fastidious manager of the marina tidied his nautical-styled cap and stood straight, as if to attention. 'I saw some strangers leave his boat,' said the eccentric, known by the residents as *The Commodore*. Whether he'd served in any naval capacity would always remain a mystery but no one really cared. He dressed in a blazer, cravat, cap and all the flamboyant nautical apparel that the amateur boatman thought was chic. Most conversations which McCabe had with him were usually long-winded and struggled to get to the point. But on this occasion he had McCabe's full attention. 'When was that?'

The Commodore flipped through his desk diary, stopped at a page and ran an index finger down the entries. 'It was the day when the maintenance people came to check the lighting on the quayside. I suppose that was nearly a week ago.'

It was more than unusual for the inquisitive *Commodore* not to challenge any face he didn't recognise, thought McCabe. As bad luck would have it, it was one of the few times he didn't. 'You didn't speak to them?' It sounded like a criticism.

The manager looked annoyed. 'No!' he snapped. 'I was busy with the maintenance guys. I guess I was a bit distracted.'

'You don't need to apologize,' replied McCabe, treading carefully.

It certainly was unusual. The manager poked his nose into almost every activity that took place in the marina but on the one occasion when it mattered, he'd done nothing,

The Commodore sensed McCabe's irritation. 'I'm sorry,' he whispered.

'Well can you describe them?' persevered McCabe.

The Commodore looked sheepish again. 'Not really.'

'What about the security CCTV?'

'It doesn't catch everything. It stays on a hard drive for a month. But I'm not sure if it would pick up any detail. You're welcome to go through it if you wish. The police didn't ask me for them.'

'The police?'

'Someone from the police rang and told me that Mr. Meyer had died in an accident.'

'Is that what they called it?' murmured McCabe.

The Commodore began to look flustered again. 'I can't remember. The policeman may have used another word but he didn't say it was murder.' He opened his desk diary again, produced a small piece of paper tucked inside the front cover. 'He said he was called Fischer, Police Chief, from St. Augustine's in Florida.'

'What else did he say?' pushed McCabe. He liked *The Commodore* but sometimes his antics and dopiness were seriously annoying.

The manager looked flustered. He was struggling to remember. 'So many things I had to deal with that day. I didn't know if he had any Russian friends.'

'What are you talking about?' McCabe shook his head. The old boy has finally flipped, he thought. He'd get no sense out of him now.

'I told him I've never met any of his friends.'

This wasn't the ranting of a senile old man. McCabe realised *The Commodore* was serious. 'He asked you if Meyer had any Russian friends? Are you sure?' prodded McCabe.

'Yes; yes I am.'

McCabe took the paper and read the scrawl carefully. Why did the Florida Police Chief ask that question? He didn't understand. 'I'll take you up on your CCTV offer. That would be good.' He still wasn't sure if the old man was raving.

In a fairly short time, the marina had changed profile enormously evolving into a relatively affluent neighbourhood from its poorer former self. The presence of CCTV was a monument to that transition. It had been a demarcation point for Union troops and the site of a military hospital during the Civil War. At the end of the Second World War it had been home to plenty of Washington's poor who lived on boats and survived off the river's produce. A serious makeover in the fifties transformed it into the home of the more prosperous; the boats in the newly developed marina equipped with all the amenities of modern living.

McCabe checked the marina CCTV footage under the attentive supervision of *The Commodore*. It wasn't a crowded video so it was easy to identify the personalities. He didn't have an accurate time of the burglary, so it was tedious trawling through the recording. In the end he got lucky. The body language of a sole hooded figure emerging from Meyer's boat gave every indication that he shouldn't have been there. But the quality of the picture was poor and the shot too far away.

At least it confirmed what he'd suspected although it didn't tell him who the intruder was, what he had been looking for or if he'd found it. He could speculate on the answers to those questions. But it gave him some encouragement. Now, he was sure he was on the right track.

Chapter 10

St. Augustine, Florida

Darlene Shannon, Coastal Intelligence Unit, pulled the telephone close to her ear while studying the latest statistics sent to her by head office. 'You could be right. It may be the cruise ship,' said the caller from Washington. 'We don't have any other evidence except her sailing patterns which might match that of *The Georgia*. They're not exactly the same but close.'

It was a long shot. In philosophical terms it was possible, albeit improbable. She hated those caveats that told her nothing. Statisticians she knew juggled figures around, some to get the results they'd already determined. In the world of uncertainty and speculation, she would have preferred them to concede that her hypothesis was at least feasible.

'What are you telling me then?' she snapped down the phone.

'Agent Shannon, all I'm saying is that it's possible,' responded the caller, sounding a little guarded.

Shannon couldn't disguise her impatience. She knew the evidence in a courtroom might be considered circumstantial but she had a feeling about this case. The *Orient Atlantic* had cropped up in her investigations too many times to be ignored. She had to press the number crunchers in the headquarters in DC to see what they could discover. The cruise ship's route, on too many occasions, crossed with that of *The Georgia* for it to be a coincidence.

As if reading her mind the caller interjected. 'What you're suggesting maybe just coincidence, you appreciate that, don't you? We've had reports of boxes loaded on other ships before but they didn't amount to anything. I'm not sure why you think they're any different.'

She found herself fighting an instinctive reaction to scream, to swear out loud, to demand the caller be more imaginative and not behave predictably like a mathematician. But that wasn't their province. Cold logic was their patch, which was why she was talking to him. She controlled her feelings, took a deep breath and said quietly. 'I'm not buying the COINCIDENCE,' she said emphasising the word. 'We're talking about the scale, the quantity, loaded onto a separate part of the ship with an obvious armed guard. Unmarked boxes and crates, not accounted for in the ship's manifest.'

The caller got the message.

'What do you want me to do then?' he said sounding totally compliant.

She had the feeling she'd overstepped the mark. The stats people in headquarters had been more than generous with their time. She didn't want to sour any relationship she had with them which had taken months to develop. 'Sorry,' she said quickly. 'Could you run a check on the passenger list for me? Thanks for your help. Humour me a little longer,' she added, attempting a smile into the phone.

'I did and we had a couple of strange results. Again I emphasise that these support possible theories. But we're a long way from hard factual evidence.'

Shannon closed her eyes and fought her instinct to fire another aggressive salvo at her statistician. She knew the stats people occupied different worlds and it was in hers that the speculation turned from theory into reality. That was her job. It was called detection. But sometimes she craved some visionary input. She suppressed her feelings again and tried to lighten up. 'I know we are coming from different places but feel free to express any of your ideas. All are welcome.' She paused a little as she said it. The last thing she desired was waves of ludicrous theories from every direction. But in this case, she did want his views. After all, he was the expert on possibilities and probabilities.

'I'd rather not, ma'am,' he said formally.

'OK, just tell me what you have,' she replied, resigned to the status quo.

'We ran some correlation software and then tried to match up those results against expectation and probability,' he said as if explaining simple arithmetic.

'Hold it there!' It sounded like a plea, more than a command.

'I thought you might want to know the process, to help you understand the results,' he said quickly, suddenly aware of her inhibitions.

'Thanks. But just tell me what you've discovered.'

'I still have to give you some idea how we arrived at our findings, don't you think? I want you to understand what I've done, so you know what the stats mean.'

'OK but please, keep it simple,' she replied almost in a whisper.

'Sorry, I guess we get carried away with our work.' It sounded like a justification. 'We don't get too many chances to talk to our agents in the field.'

'I understand.' She sounded sympathetic.

'There are a few passengers who have had repeat bookings on the *Orient Atlantic* in the last three cruises. Perhaps more but that is as far back as we checked,' he said, sounding quite excited. 'There were several women whom we suspected might be....' He hesitated. 'Who might have been, I think the phrase is, plying their trade.'

This time Shannon fought to suppress an urge to laugh out loud. She didn't think anyone used that phrase any more. Her statistician almost sounded embarrassed. How old fashioned, she thought. How endearing. 'You mean they're hookers?' she said bluntly.

'I wouldn't know anything about that,' he said quite emphatically. 'I'm told some of these repeat bookings are women just looking for company or maybe husbands,' he added, in an attempt to challenge the earlier inference.

Again she was struggling to keep a straight face. If the issue hadn't been so serious, she would have seen the humour in their conversation. 'But I can tell from your voice there are some who have caught your attention. Am I right?'

He didn't hesitate this time. 'Yes there is; one in particular. She is much younger than the rest, about mid-twenties. Travels on her own, using the same name and judging by her photograph looks...' His voice suddenly became inaudible.

'I didn't catch that,' commented Shannon loudly.

He cleared his throat, more a reflection of his embarrassment than anything else. 'Glamorous,' he said quickly.

'Glamorous?' she repeated.

He was even more uneasy now. 'I mean, some men might find her....' He stopped again, struggling to find the words.

'Sexy! Is that the description you're looking for?' she said, coming to his rescue.

He was silent for a moment, still obviously embarrassed.

'Apparently, she arrives at the ship driving a BMW sports,' he added. His response sounded a mixture of surprise and admiration.

'What else do you know about her?'

'Nothing.'

'Do you have a name?'

'Irina Lukin is the one in her passport but she uses the name May James sometimes.''

'Is she one of those ladies *plying their trade*?'

The awkward silence reappeared.

'Let's not make any assumptions then. Check her out. Is she the only rebooking?'

At the other end of the phone the young statistician typed a few instructions into his laptop and studied the results. 'Just confirming what I'd spotted earlier. Mr. Meyer has been on the cruise ship three times too, although it's not quite as clear-cut as the girl.'

Shannon rolled her eyes in despair. Not another statistical anomaly, she hoped. 'What's the problem this time?'

'I have identified him from the CCTV in the boarding area, matched against the other databases we usually check against, like passport and driver's license. He seems to try and change his appearance but it's the same man on each occasion.' The assistant was pleased with his conclusions and his summary. He felt more confident than with his previous analysis.

'You're sure?' she asked, waiting for the long-winded caveats on probability and possibility. 'Positive?' she asked, seeking confirmation.

'Definitely; it was Meyer.'

Shannon leaned back in her desk, rubbed her eyes then the back of her neck. She felt tense; a headache was on its way unless she relaxed. Her plans had gone into free fall. But they had to succeed. There was no compromise in that regard. This was her assignment and the results had to be positive. It was her instinct that had made this project fly.

Her superiors, as ever, were sceptical about an initiative coming from a woman and someone so young. Perhaps she was misjudging them? Maybe she was being obsessive? Whether it was true or not, she didn't care. That's the way she felt; the constant strain of always having to prove herself.

She'd felt that at university and at the Coast Guard training school. No nights on the dance floor and just a smattering of the communal drinks to keep her honed in the social skills she'd need on her way up the ladder. Ambitious may be an obvious trait but it was expected of her male colleagues. Why should it be considered a fault in her? It wasn't, as far as she was concerned, and no one would tell her it was inappropriate or misplaced.

The operation had been her choice, as was Meyer. He was the ideal operator for what she had in mind. His background as a yachtsman, his toughness and his military discipline were ideal; the perfect combination of skills and courage that she'd needed for this dangerous assignment. He'd been well briefed on what to expect, what the outcome needed to be and what would be required of him. He had no illusions. He'd said so. But something had gone wrong, terribly wrong. It had cost him his life. She felt for the dead man and the circumstances in which he'd died but the mission was too important to be abandoned now, particularly with the price he had paid.

'On that other matter,' the caller continued.

She braced herself for another wave of bad news.

'We didn't find it,' said the caller abruptly. 'We're not sure if he did. We have no idea if he knows what he's looking for. If he does or he finds it we may have a problem.'

'I hope you didn't leave the place....' she replied before being interrupted.

The caller knew what was coming. 'I'm only passing on the report I was given. Apparently we didn't have any choice. There's a manager in the marina who is a bit of a snoop, not in any viscious way, he just likes to keep the place in check.'

'What does that mean?'

'He's a nuisance. My report says he was beside the boat before we knew what was happening. If he hadn't been called on his cell phone and walked to the other side of the pontoon while he answered, he'd have walked in on us.'

'Did he go in, after you left?'

'No.'

'So nobody knows you've been there?'

He hesitated.

She detected the pause. 'What happened? I need to know.'

He didn't hesitate this time. 'McCabe turned up.'

'You're sure it was him?'

Again there was no hesitation. 'We'd been watching him. It was him alright; no question.'

'Did he see you?'

'No!' The answer was quite emphatic.

'He's no fool. So he now knows someone was there looking for something. And that'll also tell him it was something of importance,' she said, obviously annoyed.

'We don't know what he was after. They were neighbours. Perhaps it was a personal visit?'

She winced. Thank God the world didn't depend on this man's curiosity. The world would have remained dormant for centuries if left to his enquiring mind. The contents of McCabe's profile she'd read flashed across her mind. She could feel herself getting irritated. 'Personal thing, my ass,' she whispered to herself. 'Don't you ever think laterally?' she asked loudly. It was a serious question. She doubted she would get a thought-provoking answer 'I mean see something apart from the obvious?'

He made no sound at the other end of the phone. It told her that she had lost him again but it wasn't the telephone signal. It was the brain on the other side. That's where the connection was faulty.

She'd been trying to steer the conversation towards something meaningful. But it was difficult. 'He wasn't making a neighbourly visit.' There wasn't much more she could expect from the phone call. 'Text me your observations, I'm sure they'll be helpful,' she said, not prepared to waste any more time. She was probably being a little dismissive but she was feeling impatient and her frustration was beginning to show.

She pressed the red button on her cell phone, sighed and turned to her tablet as the text from the caller came pouring on screen. She stared at one item at the end. *I forgot to mention McCabe was on the boat for two hours.*

She was still at a loss to determine where she should go from here.

The police in St. Augustine had disclosed little about Meyer's death or the appearance of his corpse aboard the stolen yacht. She suspected they were as much in the dark as anyone else.

There was plenty of speculation, as was evident in the Florida press but nothing of substance. Some of the theories surrounding the death were fanciful; from a prison breakout to the revenge of a jealous lover. They made interesting reading and whimsical conversations in the local bars. But they didn't move the story forward in any way.

She would like to have seen Meyer's body. It might have told her nothing but somehow she felt she needed to pay her respects. She wanted to know what little the police had uncovered, if anything. But she couldn't just waltz into the local police headquarters and flash her badge. The logistics were easy but it was unlikely to produce any worthwhile results. It would also trigger a load of questions, inspire a whole new focus on the circumstances surrounding the dead body and provoke unwanted attention. She couldn't take that risk.

So far, her strategy had been to watch.

The involvement of the journalist Mike McCabe might turn out to be an unforeseen blessing. If his reputation, as the determined newshound, had any currency he might prove invaluable. The waves created by his enquiries might rock this boat in more ways than one. She'd been tempted to approach him directly but had decided otherwise. It was still a possibility. In the meantime she'd have him followed, in the hope that she'd share in any of his discoveries. At some stage, however, she knew she'd have to show her hand. Then she'd have to be certain about him and the strategy.

Chapter 11

Washington, DC

Maritime Excursions had seen better days. It looked as if in a previous life it had been a large mobile home. Given its size, in its heyday it was probably luxurious but now it no longer graced any manicured residential park but was now part of a dowdy commercial backwater about thirty miles from DC, the other residents being cheap liquor stores and motor-repair workshops.

Surprisingly, the inside of the travel agency was bright and cheerful, although tired too and in need of some tender loving care. Certainly, a coat of paint would not have gone amiss.

A lanky looking figure was squeezed behind a desk, much too small for purpose. He looked up at the noise of the door banging behind McCabe.

His smile was welcoming. He stood up and stretched to what looked like a full six and a half feet. He extended his right hand.

'Can I help you, sir?' he said, somewhat formally.

'Gary?' asked McCabe, as he took his hand.

He suddenly looked worried, as if a debtor had turned up to make a claim, but he nodded without saying anything.

McCabe sensed the mood change. He wasn't quite sure how he would tackle the next step and was banking on the agent not recognising Meyer. With a bit of luck, they'd only ever spoken on the phone. He wasn't going to try any subtle footwork but take the direct approach. 'Meyer,' he said quickly watching the salesman carefully. 'Harry,' he added immediately.

There didn't seem to be any reaction.

McCabe put the two words together and repeated them slowly. 'Harry Meyer,' he said emphasising the words carefully.

The agent still looked blank then suddenly repeated the name. 'Harry Meyer.' But he was still trying to find the connection. 'Ah yes,' he added, still sounding vague. He went back to his desk, squeezed into the seat again and punched a few commands into his computer. He studied the screen. 'I'm sorry Mr. Meyer, that place has gone. I did warn you that the offer was conditional on you confirming immediately. We can't hold vacancies. You know that from our previous dealings.'

He was right. Gary had never met Meyer. McCabe wondered if he'd learn anymore by keeping up the pretence. He decided on the opposite strategy. His reaction to Meyer's death might tell him something. 'No apology needed, Gary. My mistake; you see Harry Meyer is dead,' he said without comment. The words sounded blunt. Without any caveat, they lacked any finesse, any warmth, any regret or sympathy. They sounded like a news bulletin. He watched the salesman carefully.

Gary sank back in his chair. He looked genuinely surprised. 'I've only spoken to him on the phone a few times. I'm so sorry. I thought he was fairly young. Was he ill?' He shook his head in disbelief. 'When he didn't call back, I knew it would be something like that.'

'Did you?'

'I guessed it was something like that,' he repeated. 'How did he die?'

McCabe didn't want to get in too deep. Pursuing a conversation along those lines was pointless. The odd white lie was fine but ambiguity would suffice for now; detail was unnecessary. 'It was a surprise to everyone who knew him,' he said convincingly. 'I'm a neighbour of his in the boat community near the yacht club on the Potomac. We're all trying to clear up his affairs; ensure he didn't owe anybody. We gathered he did some business with you?' The story sounded perfectly feasible.

'And you are?'

'Sorry, Mike McCabe is my name. As I said, Harry Meyer was a neighbour.'

Gary typed vigorously on his computer again. He peered at the screen. 'The other two trips have been bought and paid for; nothing outstanding.'

'Two trips?'

'Yes,' he said as he inspected the text on the screen. 'Two trips over the last few months,' he said, touching the entries on the listing.

McCabe pulled out a small notebook. 'Just so that I can tell who may be interested. Could you give me those dates?' he said, nodding at the pad.

The agent scrolled down the displayed file a little further. 'He only went on the *Orient Atlantic*. It sails from Miami on the twelfth of every month. He's been on the last two outings. This would have been his third. Nothing owing, paid up in full with credit card. We don't hold those details; not allowed.'

'I assume he was on his own? I mean he only bought one ticket?' asked McCabe quietly, aware that he may be treading on some privacy issue.

'Yes,' said Gary, beginning to look uneasy.

McCabe sensed his discomfort. 'Sorry! We weren't sure if he had a partner who needed to be notified,' he lied.

McCabe now felt uncomfortable. He wanted to push the agent but he guessed he may have gone too far already. But he had to try. The agent was the only lead he had. 'Do you know why he went on that particular cruise ship?'

The response was a predictable silence. He HAD overstepped the mark.

'I can't tell you anything more. I've told you all I know. I'm only a travel agent, sir.'

'But didn't you think that going back on the same trip so soon was unusual?'

The agent switched off his computer. The gesture was not lost on McCabe. There was a finality to it. 'No. It's not usual at all,' he added.

Instinctively, McCabe wanted to push him even more, to sustain the momentum. But it didn't take an ace reporter to know the interview was over. He'd got all that was going and he doubted if there was much more the agent could tell anyway. He leaned across the counter and picked a brochure from the leaflet carousel. With a bit of luck, this might help fill in some details but he needed to throw the net much wider. He needed someone who could put these little clues into some perspective, help him to determine the contours of the story he was blindly chasing. That was the nature of this game; follow one hunch until the trail dried up then take a turning until it proved a dead end too. That was his type of journalism; nothing glamorous, just an endless slog of questions and answers. Eventually, if he was lucky, he'd ask the right questions and get the right answers. But even the most dedicated newshound needed a pointer and a stroke of luck.

Outside the travel office he scrolled through his cell phone directory. It had been a while since last he'd called this number. Perhaps his contact wasn't there anymore. It was the beauty of the cell phone; independent of location, the numbers seem to stay the same, despite the mobility of the owner. It rang four times before a familiar voice answered. He was in business.

Chapter 12

Washington, DC

McCabe stood in the small park at the centre of Dupont Circle, the heart of northwest Washington; an enclave of affluent middle class professionals which had become the home to many in the gay community. The transformation was evident in the growth of good restaurants, bars and fashionable outlets. They had breathed new life into an area which hadn't quite got to the ambitious heights harboured for it by its residents. But now it had arrived. The Double-Income No Children community was everywhere to be seen. There was a physical circle in which the well off and the less fortunate enjoyed its benches and occasional sunshine.

Lovers and office workers shared the seats dotted around the circular park while others played chess on the concrete boards, now a permanent feature. Some obviously homeless rummaged through the garbage bins. The comfortable and the deprived mixed with curious ease. He caught sight of Dwight Sanchez making his way across the circle towards him with his distinctive bouncing walk.

Sanchez, whose parents had slipped into the US across the Mexican border long before he was born and the restrictions were so rigid, was an extremely clever researcher and analyst. In his early thirties, he worked out of a tiny space, once used by a caretaker who kept a local apartment block functioning. Now, no longer needed, it was a small rented studio. From this modest cubbyhole, Sanchez laboured for his clients, trawling every database in the public domain and a few that were supposed to be restricted in access. He had a talent with computers which rewarded him handsomely. But it was a second life. The other hat he wore was as a civil servant, in some aspect of National Security, which McCabe sought to ignore.

McCabe had met him, by accident, while writing an article on divorce lawyers. The computer expert, from one of the Arizona universities, became a standard resource for lawyers looking for ammunition to help their clients settle a divorce favourably, usually in a way that would guarantee them the lion's share of the family assets. It was a messy business which didn't disturb the sensitivities of Sanchez too much. He burrowed through all sorts of electronic sources and soon emerged with the information needed. It was a unique second-career path that could not be found in any university vocational guidebook. Unconventional, if not marginally legal, he could tunnel his way into the most private and supposedly secure warrens of confidential information, copy what he needed and leave without anyone being the wiser.

'That's the secret,' he once told McCabe. 'Getting in is clever but getting out with the information without anyone realising you've been in there, now that's the signature of genius.'

Genius or no, McCabe felt a little uncomfortable when he had to use him. He knew he was bending the rules, if not breaking them. He tried not to think about it too much.

'What harm does it do? These are the bad guys, McCabe. I thought that's who you are after?' was the predictable plea from Sanchez. It was obvious that McCabe's sanctimonious moral postures irritated him.

McCabe knew he was lowering the barrier but he'd take it a stage at a time. Sources were always a tricky part of any journalistic picture. Whether they could be trusted or their information was credible were always fundamental questions at the heart of the relationship. The character of any source was as crucial as was the motive for disclosure. There were those who had an axe to grind, who were making an attempt to even the score or to prevent something happening. Some did it for gain; money or vanity. Each source, and the sliver of information they supplied, had to be viewed with caution. It wasn't always easy to resist, if the morsel was juicy enough. He'd messed up a few times in his early years, too keen on supporting a story he'd already written in his mind. Experience gave him battle scars, reminders that caution was needed.

McCabe distrusted the mercenary whose singular motivation was money. By definition their silence and loyalty could easily be bought by the highest bidder.

Sanchez was a complex mixture; part mercenary and part thrill junkie.

McCabe wasn't happy cultivating their relationship but he'd learned a long time ago that needs must.

The *Burrito Sunrise* was at the north side of Dupont Circle and as the name implied, a fairly modest but fun Mexican eatery, more cantina than restaurant; noisy and chaotic. Orders were being shouted from tables to waiters to kitchen. It never ceased to surprise McCabe that it worked. But it did. It was like choreographic disarray, a ballet of confusion.

It was Sanchez's favourite and he wallowed in its mayhem. He seemed comfortable there, immersed in the anonymity that the cacophony gave its clientele. There was so much action nobody focused attention on anyone. It was a circus of Mexican disorder; music, waiters, chatter, laughter and the noise level just slightly below the threshold of pain. McCabe would have preferred a place where it was easier to talk.

But it was Sanchez's choice. Given his business, it wasn't surprising that he liked the camouflage of noise. He would order his usual Beef Burrito, followed by a margarita or two to get in the mood. So far, he'd drunk two, had ordered a third and had not even tackled the menu yet. They'd only been there twenty minutes.

'Did you make any headway on the question I sent you?' asked McCabe, more than anxious to get the Mexican's show on the road. He'd the basic PR blurb on Meyer but he needed more. Sanchez smiled broadly and beckoned the waiter. He ordered a Beef Burrito and another margarita as he slugged down the last of his drink. He looked pleased with himself.

McCabe ordered a Taco and another Black Label.

'Yes I did,' said Sanchez slowly, pulling out a small notebook. He flipped through a few pages quickly, scanning the contents as he went. His eyes ran down the notes on each page and he nodded in confirmation. 'Your man led an interesting life or should I say several?'

McCabe said nothing as he studied the Mexican's face. He liked him, albeit with obvious reservations. The information he'd provided on previous occasions, although traded would be a better description, was always reliable.

He waited until Sanchez resettled. After the margarita infusions visibly began to take effect, he was good to go again.

'How much did you know about this man?' said Sanchez, as he leaned back into his chair.

McCabe looked slightly irritated. He wasn't going through another negotiating loop so that the price would go up. 'I told you all I know. He was a neighbour of mine in the Potomac Marina beside the Yacht Club. I barely spoke to the man in the few years I've been a resident. He was in the Navy. That's it.' He sounded annoyed and impatient.

'But he was shot dead in Florida and had your hotel details on him?'

'Yes, yes,' replied McCabe, getting more impatient.

'Sorry, Mike. I forget things, now and again.'

McCabe shook his head. 'That's reassuring,' he said with a frustrated sigh.

Sanchez laughed. 'I don't concentrate enough,' he insisted.

McCabe looked at the Tequila and the now three empty glasses lined up across the table. 'I wonder what could be the cause of that?' he said, nodding towards the glasses.

'He was not an easy man to check on,' restarted Sanchez. He flipped through a few more notebook pages, stopped at one then read it.

'I don't want to be burdened by the logistics, just tell me what you found out,' insisted McCabe.

Sanchez shook his head. 'Nothing, well not much.'

'Tell me what you have.'

Sanchez flipped through his notebook again and shook his head. 'It tells me that this man is government.'

'What does that mean?' snapped McCabe. 'I don't want any speculation. I can do that myself.'

Sanchez looked offended. 'I'm trying to help you here, using my experience.'

'Sorry,' murmured McCabe. 'I appreciate that but I need facts.'

Sanchez focused on one page and read from his notebook. 'He was in the US Navy for over ten years but then appeared to retire with rank of captain.'

'What do you mean appeared to retire?'

Sanchez looked a little unsure. 'You don't want me to speculate, so I won't.'

McCabe said nothing for a moment. 'You're right. I think your opinion would be worthwhile. Tell me what you think.'

The Mexican turned to another page. 'I think it's obvious. A schoolboy could come up with as good a guess, as I'm sure you could. I think he became an operator, probably for a government agency.'

'Navy intelligence? What?'

'Could be any manner of related covert activity whatever national security calls itself these days but that's my guess, no fact to support the theory.'

Sanchez had another inspection of his notes. He flipped to and fro through the pages checking one page against another. 'For what it's worth, he's an expert sailor, I mean seaman or at least was.'

'Aren't they all sailing experts in the navy?'

'This guy was from the old school. He could handle anything under sail, in fact anything that floated.' He thumbed through the notebook again, then from between one of the pages pulled out a photocopy of a cutting from a magazine or newspaper. The image was crumpled too and the photo was cracked in places but the reproduction still showed a proud Meyer aboard a yacht, amidst the winner's spray from a shaken oversized magnum of champagne. He handed the image to McCabe.

'He'd won a few competitions as a skipper of racing crafts. He was a superb yachtsman. Whatever he was doing might have had that connection. That's as certain as anything'.

McCabe took the picture and studied the photo. The bronzed happy image of the man on the deck was a far cry from the pale and bruised corpse he'd seen on a police slab. He shuddered a little at the thought. 'Can I keep this?'

'Of course,' replied Sanchez, taking the picture, folding it and handing it back. 'One more thing; this is another bit of speculation but whatever this guy's game was he was good at it.' McCabe said nothing but watched Sanchez flip to the last page of his notebook. 'I wasn't able to get the details since it was wrapped up in the usual military secrecy but this man was a hero,' he added, sounding impressed.

'What makes you say that?'

'As I said, I didn't get the details but he's been decorated several times,' he added then went silent. 'My contact guessed it was some covert operation.'

That new tranche of information was alarming. In some ways it pointed the story in a different direction altogether. Covert meant government, it meant an unclear agenda where nothing was what it appeared to be.

'He needed to change his identity, if that was the case. If he did, it would be proof that he was involved in covert operations. You don't buy a new life at Walmart. Big strings need to be pulled by powerful people.' Sanchez had another swig of his drink; the hand holding his glass was noticeably shaking. He'd suddenly become more nervous. He looked towards the exit then gestured that he wanted a refill.

McCabe signalled the waiter immediately.

Sanchez was now running scared of something.

'So, we're back to speculation again?' said McCabe glibly, trying to lighten the tone.

Sanchez looked annoyed at the comment. 'Most of this is classified. I'm not giving you stats on parking fines.' There was no ambiguity in his voice; he was agitated.

McCabe felt perhaps the comment was too sharp. It wasn't intended the way it had sounded. It was always a difficult line to walk; when to press and when to back off. 'Sorry, forget that.'

'You should be careful where you're treading,' said Sanchez. It sounded like a serious warning. 'If it is security that is involved, they're not playing games. Somebody has been killed already and he had some prominence. You my friend wouldn't bother them in the slightest. Don't underestimate them.'

'I'm not quite sure I know what you're trying to tell me here.'

Sometimes Sanchez was difficult to read, particularly when he'd consumed a few. But he also had a tendency to talk in code; signals that were meant to signify something but they were not always clear.

In the past, on more than one occasion McCabe had found himself reliving a conversation with Sanchez to try and detect the signals and interpret their meaning.

McCabe had a feeling this could be one of those.

'When this type of mess erupts, there's some underlying conflict, could be within the agencies themselves. But that's another piece of guesswork.' Sanchez didn't say another word but rose from the table quietly, nodded with a smile and left. That was the way it had always been. When he wanted to leave, he was gone.

McCabe watched him negotiate his way, rather uncertainly, up the small stairwell and through the exit door. The facts disclosed were hardly earth shattering but they did give some idea of the company the dead man might have been keeping. It gave no clue to why he'd been murdered. Clearly, it wasn't because of any lack of sailing prowess or bravery.

Sanchez's warnings were worth noting. The Mexican was no longer in his prime but he was still tuned into the vagaries of covert government and even fuelled with the courage of several margaritas, his conjecture had some currency. Only a fool would ignore it.

Chapter 13

Washington, DC

McCabe was at National Airport in Washington well ahead of schedule. Like plenty of others in the departure lounge, he was on his tablet catching up on the world. He was old enough to remember when radio was the only immediate medium for news. Now it poured from every electronic outlet with too much of it having no substance whatsoever. He checked his email to see if the news desk in Washington had any messages or updates. He scoured a few professional data bases; also nothing. The story of dead Meyer hadn't moved forward. The police still hadn't issued any statement. Fischer was on air repeating what he'd been saying for the last several days; the police were investigating, the dead man found on board the yacht was the victim of a shot to the head. There was no evidence to indicate who the assailant might be.

However there was one interesting development. On one news channel a very articulate and slick young women from Coast Guard Intelligence claimed that the yacht was known to the authorities but would not be drawn further.

He was so involved in his web trawling that he almost missed his flight. On its last call, the airline mentioned him by name. He raced to the gate and sneaked onto the aircraft, a little sheepishly, as he faced the obvious annoyance of his waiting fellow passengers. He smiled benignly to those whose eyes he couldn't avoid and settled in for the short flight to Daytona Beach. In his haste, his tablet and iphone were in the hand-luggage locker overhead. The last thing he wanted to do was disturb anyone again by trying to retrieve them. From inside his jacket pocket, he pulled out the travel agent's brochure on the *Orient Atlantic*. That would have to do.

From the photo on the front cover, the ship looked enormous. He didn't know anything about these maritime giants but, even to his untrained eye, it looked like a floating city. It claimed to have fifteen decks and to carry a staggering five and a half thousand passengers. Food and entertainment by the ton was its hallmark. He shook his head, in a mixture of admiration and disapproval. It was certainly not his bag. But he was part of a minority. The cruise ship travel trade was booming, prepared in their floating heavens to satisfy almost all appetites of the young and old; no expense spared. It sounded clichéd but judging by the illustrations, it seemed real enough.

He guessed he was old-fashioned. His idea of a vacation was to go to a town he'd never visited before, preferably with some history, meander into its unfashionable back waters, discover local places to drink and eat, all in an effort to sample its hidden culture. Not that he'd taken many vacations, if any, in the last few years.

But where was the culture aboard a tailor-made floating luxury hotel? Where were the covert recesses of historical interest? Where would he find tradition in gleaming modern surroundings? He sighed as he counted the decks and shook his head in disapproval again. The list of the entertainment and facilities were long and impressive. The photos showed everyone was in some state of rapture.

McCabe knew he was being cynical. Had Harry Meyer been one of those who had an insatiable appetite for this nautical Shangri-La and its exotic promise?

He didn't know Meyer at all but he didn't think so. His houseboat wasn't full of memorabilia from his previous cruises. Had it not been for the telephone message, there was no indication that Meyer had any interest in the ship at all. Perhaps there was an innocent reason for the cruises, simply in search of companionship? Meyer lived alone and the booking had been made solely for him. Was the explanation that simple?

Normally that would have been a perfectly reasonable explanation. But three trips in as many months didn't ring true. This was a man who had been found barely a week ago with a bullet in his brain, on the deck of an unmanned stolen yacht which was drifting into a busy tourist haunt on the east coast of northern Florida. That defied any reasonable explanation.

Of course, the cruises might have no bearing on Meyer's death at all. There was no evidence to suggest that they were related. But in search of any story, the fundamentals were always worth exploring. It was good advice and it was always a reliable pointer.

He turned to the back of the brochure. The Bahamas and Cuba were the main places where the ship docked, two of the most popular destinations for most of the liners based in Miami. Did these places have any significance to the story he was chasing? The principle of cause and effect here might be irrelevant; rational and profound analysis didn't always work with human nature.

But he was convinced there must be a connection, no matter how obscure, between one piece of this jigsaw and another. Among this jumble of pieces was a catalyst which would make the blurred picture become clearer. Finding it was part of the challenge.

The Delta flight from DC now bumped its way along the runway at Daytona Beach Airport. McCabe needed a drink and fast. Fortunately the bar was still open and quiet. He ordered a double Black Label and relaxed.

Where his story went from here, he didn't know. The cruise ship was an important backdrop certainly but where Meyer's yacht had sailed would be crucial in knowing the reason for the poor man's murder.

It was a nice warm Floridian evening when he emerged from the terminal. There was a hint of a cool breeze that made the air less balmy. He jumped into a cab and headed back to another hotel on the St. Augustine waterfront. Was he imagining things or was there a car following him?

He shouted to the cab driver to take a quick left. The car behind tried to make the same turn but misjudged the traffic signals. The driver soon found himself marooned in the middle of the junction, surrounded by honking impatient traffic.

McCabe was right. He was being followed.

Chapter 14

St. Augustine, Florida

Fischer opened the door to the forensic lab slowly. At the far end he caught sight of Barrett, head of forensic, supping coffee and eating what looked like a bagel, as if he were relaxing on his front porch.

Despite years of experience, Fischer hated the lab. The smell of bleach, formaldehyde and the sickly unmistakable odour of blood was a cocktail he found nauseating. He couldn't understand how Barrett could eat in such surroundings.

'Always good to see you here, Chief,' said the forensic holding up his cup in salute. 'Would you like one?'

Fischer shook his head. 'No,' he answered quickly.

'Why do I get the impression you don't like being here? I would have thought that after all these years....'

Fischer interrupted him. 'Doctor, I don't have a lot of time,' he said impatiently.

'I take it that's a no then?' Barrett said with a laugh. 'Sorry, Chief. There's plenty if you change your mind.'

Fischer tried to force a smile. He wasn't too convincing.

Barrett finished his coffee, moved to his desk, keyed a few instructions into his computer, put on a pair of spectacles, scanned the screen then started reading from it. 'Just a quick recap, so there are no gaps. His name is Harry Meyer, in his early sixties, sixty three to be precise. The tattoo about *God and the Sea*, you remember.'

'Did you decipher anything else?'

Barrett shook his head and sighed a little. 'There was nothing that would help you, Chief. There was an anchor design and more barely readable lettering. As best as I could decipher, it looked like ANGEL. But that was it.'

Fischer sat on a chair opposite the forensic. 'I was hoping for more.'

Barrett looked annoyed. 'We're scientists, Chief. We don't perform miracles,' he said with a laugh.

Fischer didn't react. He obviously didn't share the joke.

'I don't mean to be frivolous,' continued Barrett, trying to lighten the atmosphere. 'We now know from the fingerprints we took that there were dozens of others on board at some time or other. That means nothing and tells us nothing, except that the yacht had a crew. Or, at least, usually did. I'm discounting the new prints from the party-boarders.'

'I gather Meyer was quite an accomplished sailor and could have handled the boat himself,'

'Yes, but let me finish. We went through the basic checks on everything on board again; just to ensure we hadn't missed anything.'

Fischer seemed to brighten up a little. 'And?'

'There were no documents aboard that identified Meyer at all. Either he didn't have any when he boarded the vessel or they had been removed. He was wearing a lifejacket, so he was dressed for a sail. There is plenty of fresh water on board but not a lot of food. What does that tell us?'

'That he may have left in a hurry?'

'Or a journey that was opportune. He didn't have too much time to plan.'

'Why do you say that?'

'There were some men's clothes aboard. We checked the sizes, some could have been his, some not.'

'What are you telling me then?'

'As I said, it does suggest he left in a hurry, an opportunity arose and he took it. The reason behind that quick exit, well, that's your job, remember.'

Fischer stood up and turned towards the door. He'd heard enough. The forensic findings didn't take the story much further. He looked disappointed.

Barrett kept talking. 'There was an inflated dinghy, secured on deck. I'm not sure what that tells us, either. Perhaps he expected trouble or was in the process of abandoning ship. Who knows? We don't have too much to go on.'

Fischer was now half way to the door. 'What about that cigarette you found?'

Barrett's eyes widened. 'I'd forgotten about that,' he said going back to his file. 'I was right, east European. It's difficult to tell given its condition but it could be a Sobranie, although we don't know how old it is.'

'That confirms Russian then?'

'Well, yes and no. Originally they were made in Russia but then in Britain and now they're owned by the Japanese. Who the smoker was is anyone's bet. But it wasn't Meyer. His lungs were in great shape for his age, no teeth stains or gum issues. He wasn't a smoker.'

Fischer slowly walked the rest of the way to the door.

'You're always in a hurry, Chief. Hear me out,' commented Barrett, sounding a little frustrated trying to get attention from the wandering policeman.

Fischer stopped quickly.

Barrett pressed another few keys then read from the screen. It was a blog written by someone on another yacht. The blog had been reported in an electronic newspaper which exchanged gossip, hints and tittle-tattle about yachting at sea. A chance encounter by a family on a sailing trip claimed in the article they'd posted on their travel blog, that they'd seen *The Georgia* sailing south of them about fifty miles north of Saint Augustine. The yacht, barely half a mile from them in the early evening, appeared to be sailing normally. It wasn't drifting but was in danger of moving into a commercial shipping channel. They signalled with a flashlight to alert the yacht but got no reply. Their concern was it could easily drift into the path of a cargo ship or liner in the dark. They doubted whether, like their vessel, it would show up on a ship's radar and so would run the risk of collision. After several attempts they went on about their business and didn't think anything of it until they heard the radio reports about the drifting yacht and the dead man aboard. They contacted the Coast Guard immediately.

Barrett stared at the computer and peered at the last line of the text. 'It's timed just before sundown about two days before *The Georgia* turned up here.'

'Can you run me off a copy?' asked Fischer still in thought.

The forensic nodded, pulled a file from under a pile of paperwork, opened it and selected a sheet from inside the sheath. 'I've done that already. Thought you might want one. The quality isn't too good, I'm running low on ink but you can read it easily enough,' he said handing Fischer the sheet.

The policeman scanned the article quickly. 'What's your take on this then? It doesn't identify the yacht.'

'It's *The Georgia* alright,' insisted Barrett.

'Was Meyer dead then?'

The forensic nodded in agreement. 'If he was alive, he was shot shortly after that. The sighting is roughly our estimated time of death.'

'They didn't see him or anyone else on board?'

'No!'

'Anything else?' asked Fischer, sounding frustrated again. There was a definite change in his voice.

Barrett detected it. 'Not a great report, I'll grant you. We have his fingerprints, a copy of his driver's license, a passport and an address in DC, no next of kin and a very basic outline of the work he did. That's it.'

The policeman looked puzzled again. 'I spoke to the marina where he lived but nothing there either.' He shook his head and sighed. 'He's a high ranking naval officer, awarded medals supposedly for bravery, but there are no published details of his citations; strange.'

'That's not unusual,' insisted Barrett.

'Only if he's been on secret missions; otherwise they scream from the rooftop, don't they?'

The forensic shook his head. 'I don't know. But what I found curious is that he leaves the service and there is no information on the circumstances.' Barrett was back on his computer with another few keyboard instructions. 'He was in the US navy, a high ranking expert in navigation, and then he leaves with no reason given. He wasn't drilled out or anything. Maybe he didn't leave?'

'What does that mean?' quizzed Fischer.

'What I mean is, his record has died, stopped, there's nothing more. Do we have to assume he left. Or do we?'

'What else can we assume?'

Barrett shrugged his shoulders.

'I know you're a scientist; you only deal in facts,' Fischer said as he walked behind Barrett to read the computer screen again. 'But there is something contrived about his profile, as if it had been manufactured. I can't put my finger on it.'

'If I had to guess....' said Barrett. He stopped typing and looked at Fischer, as if waiting for approval.

The policeman nodded. 'OK; let's have it.'

'I'd say it is contrived; PR, meant to be read.'

'What does that mean?' fired Fischer. 'I don't follow.'

'It's what he's done at the end of this biography I'd like to know about. Whatever it is, clearly it's concealed or at least not made public. It raises the obvious question; why?'

Chapter 15

St. Augustine, Florida

The drive to St. Augustine took longer than normal. On route, McCabe had counted at least half a dozen camper vans or whatever they called them in this part of the world. It was a type of vacation that never appealed to him; it was barely above living out of a small suitcase in a downmarket hotel. He had to admit he was spoiled. He'd almost forgotten the tacky tourist hotels he'd been forced to frequent over the years. Either he had got more affluent or the standards had got higher. He'd probably got soft.

He pulled into his hotel not far from the waterfront; one of an international chain that looked much the same as they did in almost every city in the US. Still, there was always an overlarge bed, a million towels and many dozen television channels, although few worth watching. However, there was always a well stocked drinks cabinet at the far end of the room. He carelessly threw his bags down by the bed, opened the bar and poured himself a scotch. There was no Black Label. The ordinary Johnny Walker miniatures would have to do. He felt his ears tingle as the drink hit the back of his throat.

He pulled open the curtains and the veranda door. The sun was hot but a cool breeze from the ocean invited him to sit and savour the moment. He really needed time to try and put the pieces together. That was the usual routine; look at the bits to see if they formed any pattern, if there was any link between one clue and another.

That description was very loose. They weren't clues to anything; certainly not identifiable bits which would link together and form a recognisable pattern. Within a few minutes he was back in the room for a refill.

He leaned back in a chair and let the sun through the window hit his face. It felt good. He sipped the scotch and wondered if this story was worth pursuing at all. He didn't know why he felt compelled. Was it because Meyer had been a neighbour? That was nonsense, since he didn't remember anything that could be described as a conversation with him. Perhaps a neighbourly wave from his houseboat as McCabe walked along the pontoon had unwittingly cemented a relationship? He thought not.

But that aside, the man was dead. He was a murder victim, alone and afloat on a stolen boat that appeared to have concealed as many secrets as the dead man. And of course there was the newspaper cutting, discovered beside the body, with McCabe's hotel room number written on it. The police considered that to be significant. The truth was they were grasping at straws and were as much in the dark as anyone. Perhaps the cutting was Meyer's legacy. He knew he could be murdered and, in that event, McCabe would be the man to investigate. He shook his head. That was fantasy. The sun and the scotch were taking its toll. He felt sleepy and let his body drift.

The telephone in the room woke him. As he picked it up, he glanced at his watch. He'd been asleep for an hour. By the time he'd managed to croak some sort of answer the line went dead. A quick cool shower did its job. He was back in the land of the living and still dripping when the phone rang again.

It was the front desk. 'Mr. McCabe, you had a call earlier and I put it through but you didn't answer.' He sounded apologetic. 'I've only been in the job a few days and I'm sorry if.......'.
McCabe interrupted. 'No need. I wasn't expecting a call.' He laughed; how unusually diligent, he thought. It was probably the wrong room anyway. He hadn't finished dressing when there was a knock on the door, not a gentle humble enquiry made by a hotel employee but an assertive thump that was determined to be answered. He pulled open the door quickly in obvious annoyance. An expletive was in mid breath. He stopped quickly, his face distorted in complete surprise.

'Nearly caught you there McCabe; don't you ever answer your phone?'' said his visitor, as she leaned against the door frame. 'Close your mouth or you'll catch a fly, as my mum used to tell me. You wouldn't have a drink for a girl would you?'
McCabe closed the door, shaking his head and still not believing.

'Well, McCabe. Where's my frigging drink. That's no way to treat a lady.'

He walked quickly to the drinks cabinet. 'Scotch or bourbon?' he asked while scanning the bottle display.

She moved towards him, took a Johnny Walker miniature, poured all of it into one of the glasses on top of the cabinet, lifted it to the light, as if to inspect it and handed it to him.

'A couple of ice cubes would go down well. I always forget how frugal you Brits are with your ice.'

'Scotch should be drunk neat,' he said dropping two cubes into the glass. 'You can have more, if you like,' he said with a snigger.

She sat on the sofa and put her feet on the table.

'Tracy Garrison,' he said slowly. 'What the hell are you doing here?'

She ignored the question.

'Tracy Garrison,' he repeated, as he threw in a few more ice cubes into her glass.

'What am I doing here?' she said finishing his question. 'I could ask you the same.'

He put on his formal voice. It didn't sound convincing. 'I'm on vacation.'

She took a swig from the glass and a long drag at her roll-up.

'Crap; total crap McCabe.'

'What?'

'You've never taken a vacation in your life,' she said, taking another mouthful of scotch.

She hadn't changed much, just as sassy as he remembered her. He chuckled to himself. It was good to know that some things in life don't change. In her case that wasn't entirely true. She was mercurial and not in any way predictable. But he found her refreshing.

'What are you smiling at McCabe?'

He paused for a moment. 'Be straight with me. What are you doing here?'

She still didn't answer. Her distinctive studded leather jacket, cowboy boots, denim shorts and long dark hair would stop most men in mid-conversation. She was the epitome of a gentleman's centrefold, although the current political climate had dispensed with the term and even the reference. The ethos was still true. Whatever the political correctness of the term, she was a showstopper.

'Still working for the local paper in Daytona Beach?' He'd met her a year or so before as she trawled her patch on an old Harley Davison and lived in a restored nineteen-fifty's Winnebago. They'd had a brief affair; once met never forgotten. She was a character, cocky, tough and good at what she did.

'I'm on a sort of roving freelance contract,' she said handing him back her empty glass.

He'd toyed with the idea of freelance on more than one occasion, liberated from the burden of pursuing stories he'd written a dozen times before and not having to sell an idea to a newly appointed teenage news-editor. However, he soon dismissed the idea just as quickly. He now had the best of both worlds; a steady income with someone to pick up the expenses and a mandate to pursue stories based on his own judgement. Occasionally he'd have to fight his corner but generally he was left alone to follow his instincts. On a few occasions he envied those with complete freedom. But it was an attitude of mind. Perhaps that's why he'd always liked Tracy Garrison. He smiled again at the memory of their first meeting, the sight of her astride her Harley Davison, a present from her lover.

'What about the boyfriend then?' he asked cautiously.

For an intelligent gal she'd picked a short straw in that social category. The boyfriend had robbed a Seven-Eleven and had run out of gas while making his getaway on his Harley. You really couldn't make it up. The first time McCabe had heard the story, he couldn't keep a straight face. The great robber went to prison. The upside was he'd given his bike to her and she lived in his Winnebago while he was serving his time.

'I told you he was a nice guy but a total loser,' she said as she watched McCabe pour another drink for her. 'He got out for good behaviour then accidently set fire to the 'bago; drunk as a skunk of course. Talk about shit for brains. When they were dishing out the grey matter, he was way down the line, about three steps behind your average moron.'

'So, you left.'

'I was on my way out anyway. But he let me keep the Harley. I told you he was a nice guy.'

'You still haven't told me why you're here?' he asked cautiously. 'What's the story?' He stopped and stared at her for a moment. 'I'll buy you dinner, if you tell,' he added with a grin.

She sipped her drink for a moment. 'In that case; *The Georgia*,' she said quietly. 'I read your article on Meyer. I'm guessing you're here after the same thing.'

Chapter 16

St. Augustine, Florida

The *Lobster Pot* was a quaint intimate restaurant, tucked away in a small back street of St. Augustine but its tiny roof terrace still afforded a view over the waterfront. There was barely room for more than half a dozen tables in the small space but the one nearest the outside wall was the perfect vantage point for a breathtaking view of the harbour at sunset. McCabe knew the proprietor and had secured the coveted spot.

There was no dress code. Just as well, McCabe thought, as Tracy Garrison wearing her signature leather jacket and fashionably tattered shorts slid into the seat.

'It's called trending,' she said continuing the conversation she'd started in the street.

He was half listening as he beckoned the waiter, pointed to Black Label on the drinks menu. 'Two,' he mouthed then turned back to his guest.

'Did you hear what I said?' she quizzed.

'I thought I'd get our order in quickly. I know how impatient you get when you haven't a drink.'

'Your romantic silver tongue is really impressive,' she quipped. 'Have you been working on that?' She couldn't resist a sneaky smile.

McCabe chuckled at the not unexpected remark. It was in character. 'As a matter of fact, I have', he said, sustaining the joke.

The whiskies arrived. 'Good to see you,' he said quickly, clicking his glass on hers.

She had her first mouthful.

'Trending; that's what you said. I can't say I understand the term much. It seems to vary depending on who uses it. In my day it was synonymous with being fashionable.'

'How many hundred years ago was that McCabe?' she said. It was her turn to chuckle.

He finished his whisky, beckoned the waiter again and ordered two more. 'Make them large ones. The first ones hardly touched the sides.'

He should have remembered. When first he'd met her in Daytona Beach about two years before, she'd taken him to a local bar where their whisky, of indeterminate provenance, was strictly for the seasoned drinkers. The remainder of that evening was a little fuzzy.

She wasn't affected by the experience one bit; an old hand.

If his memory was correct, he'd had a ride on the back of her Harley when they'd emerged from the bar and then woke up beside her in the Winnebago.

'Are you getting mean in your old age?' she commented. 'That was a pitiful order you made there,' she added with a wink and a smirk. 'Only teasing,' she giggled while looking at the menu. 'I know you're a generous old gent,' she continued with the tease.

'Less of that or you'll be looking at the Wendy's to-go menu.' The new drinks arrived and she took no time in taking her first sample. 'Trending,' she said, steering the conversation back to the beginning again. 'In modern parlance, like now in the twenty-first century that is, means stories whose origins have come from social media.'

McCabe sipped his scotch and said nothing. He looked the perfect pupil.

'I can tell you're paying attention,' she commented with another chuckle. 'Excellent.'

He suddenly looked a little serious. 'That's what brought you here, to St. Augustine?'

She detected a change in his mood. 'Yes,' she replied quickly. 'No joking this time.'

Although appearing cavalier and carefree, he knew she was focused and dedicated. When she put her mind to something she was determined, if not obsessive. As he knew, she was damn good at what she did. 'Where does *The Georgia* fit into all this?'

She didn't respond to the question, instead returned to the menu. 'I'm going to have the lobster. I'll start with the soup, the chowder.'

McCabe scoured the menu quickly. 'I'll go with that too,' he said.

'Not very imaginative, McCabe.'

'And a bottle of their best Chablis; I recommend.' He called over the waiter and ordered.

By this time, the sun was setting and the predictable yet impressive kaleidoscope of shades was sprawling across the horizon. He pointed towards it but said nothing.

She nodded back. They sat in silence for a moment or two. Suddenly, as if moving into a different gear she spoke again. 'Since I've gone freelance I've picked up a lot of my stories on social media. I know you're an old fashioned hack and a damn good one who has walked the beat and done your share of foot-in-the-door stuff. But there's a whole new world out there now that talks to each other. You'd be surprised at the stories in the chatter.'

McCabe looked unimpressed. 'Loads think they're journalists. All sorts of crap, lies, innuendos and dangerous rubbish are published on social media.'

'Sure,' she responded quickly. 'But don't dismiss it. It's no different from the same fiction that politicians and their PR people peddle every day. That's when the hack wades in and deciphers what is crap. You still need that eye.'

He didn't look convinced.

Nevertheless, she sensed she was making ground. 'They use blogs and Facebook and the like to share their experiences. Some are private but some like to tell the world.'

He laughed, the tone was meant to be mocking. 'That's an endorsement of their credibility?'

She looked annoyed. 'Don't be such an old-fashioned asshole McCabe,' she said then smiled. 'I'm trying to educate you and lead you to the promised land.'

He shook his head and laughed again. He wasn't going to win this contest. 'OK; *The Georgia*?'

The conversation was interrupted by the arrival of the wine. McCabe smacked his lips with approval after a sample. 'That's fine,' he said, watching the waiter pour them each a glass.

'Before we progress, McCabe; are you going to share what you know?' she asked quietly.

He looked a little uncomfortable at the question. It was never something he'd agree to easily.

'I know you'd need to be dragged screaming into any agreement like that; part of your old fashioned livery, eh?'

'I'm after *The Georgia* story too. That's what I do, remember?' he said enjoying his first glass of the Chablis. 'How did you know I was interested?'

She laughed out loud. 'Part of your charm, McCabe, has always been your ability to make waves. The rats go scurrying for cover everywhere you go.'

'I've been making waves?'

'That's your signature. I just followed the dead bodies.'

He looked confused. 'I thought we were talking social media?'

'I know everyone in this town, the strangers, the tourists, the hustlers, the hookers; that's what I do. This is my patch, my manor, remember?'

'So?'

She stood up from the table, went to the window and gently pushed the curtain aside. 'You've been watched. I don't know for how long but he was easy for me to spot.'

McCabe walked quickly to the curtain, peered over her hand and through the window.

She dropped the curtain. 'He's not there anymore. But you can take my word for it.'

McCabe looked cynical. 'What did he look like?'

'Well, don't believe me. I don't care.' She sounded as if she meant it.

'Who was he? You said you knew everyone in the neighbourhood.'

She nodded and smiled. 'I know he's not local, neither is the woman he reported to.'

'Woman?' he repeated.

'Is there a fucking echo in here?' she said with a laugh. 'I see you still have that maddening habit of repeating things. Yes, the guy watching you reported to some dame, tall, elegant, sophisticated; not your type, too classy for you McCabe.'

'You don't know who she is either; so much for your local knowledge?'

'She's either police or the like. She was packing. I could tell the way she held herself.'

'Could you?'

'Yeah; we girls can tell those things, didn't you know? So what's a girl like her having you tailed and armed to the teeth? Not another jilted lover, McCabe. You really have to be more sensitive,' she replied with another mischievous grin.

'Talking about maddening habits. I see you still have your tawdry sense of humour.' He felt compelled to get a gibe in too.

'Perhaps, McCabe, perhaps.'

'*The Georgia*,' he said yet again, as they returned to the table. He was interrupted by the waiter who flitted and fussed for several minutes serving dinner. At last they were alone again.

'I told you, social media. I picked up the story just by chance. There is a website, an electronic magazine that I regularly monitor. They have a number of readers who submit their blogs or write articles to supplement their daily diaries. There was one by the mother of a family on a sailing trip who ran into a yacht, apparently adrift about fifty miles north of St.Augustine. They signalled the yacht but there was no response. I thought nothing of it until I saw the television reports about *The Georgia*.' She slipped her hand below the table, produced a sheet of paper and handed it to McCabe. 'That's a copy of her article, at least what was published. We'll chat about it when we've finished dinner. I'm famished.'

Enchanted by the food and mesmerized by the final stages of the sunset, they didn't say much for a while.

'Liquors are always the ideal accompaniment to a great meal,' he said, scanning the menu again. 'Don't you think?'

'I'm having another whisky,' she said signalling to the waiter.

'OK, you've sold me. I'll go with that too,' he said, as he flipped through the article she'd given him. It didn't say much more than she'd said. The family on a sailing trip had been filing a daily blog, largely to keep their two children interested and as an added safety feature.'

'I suppose, knowing that people are aware of where you are can be comforting?'

'I can tell you're not really a sailor, McCabe. No unbridled desire to explore the high seas?'

'I'll remind you that I live on a houseboat,' he said, going along with the taunt.

'Charlie Banks told me you'd say that.'

'You've seen him?'

'Of course, everybody talks to Charlie. He's a fixture. That's how I knew you were on the case and about the *Waverley Princess*.' She laughed out loud yet again. 'I told you. This is my manor. I know everybody.'

McCabe ignored the jibe and studied the printout again. 'But we don't know it was *The Georgia*.'

'No but the timings match, if what she says is accurate and those from the television reports. I know it's not concrete but it feels right. It's not the first time you've followed a story with nothing but a hunch to lead you, McCabe. You've built a reputation on less.'

He was back on the Black Label which had just arrived. 'So that's it; a hunch?' He sounded irritated. 'So what happened to the lessons on the value of social media? In the end we're down to a good old fashioned hunch?'

She sensed his annoyance and touched his arm gently. 'There's always stuff never published. I'm going to check. That's got to be worth a look. I'm going to check that out. Come with me.'

Chapter 17

St. Augustine, Florida

It was a change waking up beside her in a large hotel bed instead of the more cramped accommodation of her Winnebago. She was up, dressed and halfway through breakfast while he was still trying to kick his body into gear. 'What's the hurry?'
'Time is money; isn't that what they say?' she said with a mouthful of breakfast.
'Who the hell are they?'
'I ordered us some coffee and bagels. Early birds catch the worms, remember?'
'What the hell is this, cliché day?' he said sounding a little tetchy and rubbing his eyes. Sometimes he found her irritating. This was one such occasion. He hadn't quite got his act together yet.
Before long, still trying to finish a bagel, he was on the back of her Harley. It took them less than thirty minutes to cover a hair-raising forty miles from the coast to a rundown commercial complex, the home of the maritime blog publisher. The entire area, about the size of a small shopping mall, was full of dowdy little units housing everything from insurance brokers, photographers, car repair workshops, small printing companies and the maritime blog publisher. It didn't seem to have a name just an address. They suspected the address was used for a number of modest enterprises.

They'd barely stopped when she'd slipped from the bike and was at what purported to be the front desk. 'Sorry,' said the old man at the counter. 'Can't help you much; it's just a teenage kid who puts it together on a computer in the backroom. People just come in and put their blogs on it. There's no security or anything.'

Garrison flashed her Press Card. 'He published a blog a few days ago, I wanted to know if there was any more detail. I'm following up on a story,' she added, walking on without giving any more detail. 'This is a colleague,' she added, nodding in McCabe's direction.

He nodded back but felt it was a pretty low-key introduction.

The old man hadn't even looked at Garrison's credentials. She could have flashed anything.

He didn't seem to care. 'You won't need a password,' he said, as she passed.

'Impressive security,' murmured McCabe.

'Shut up,' she said. With that, she'd slipped into the back room and was on the computer in a matter of seconds. She didn't seem inhibited about privacy or data protection or any obvious legislation meant to ensure civil rights.

McCabe leaned over her shoulder and watched as she interrogated one file after another betwixt the occasional expletive. 'Don't you think we should be.........' he attempted to say.

'Shut up, McCabe,' she said again, barely turning towards him. 'Try not to be an asshole today.'

He shook his head; again this was an argument he wasn't going to win.

'There it is,' she shouted. 'It's about three times the length of the blog that was posted. She pressed a few more keys on the computer and checked that a copy had been captured on her phone. Satisfied, she closed down the computer.' Good, I've got it. Let's go.'

With that she was out of the office, past the counter, given a quick thank you, was out of the front door, had kick-started the Harley and was on the move. 'Are you coming McCabe? We're done!' The bike roared down the road towards the freeway, back to St. Augustine.

Flagler College is eye-catching from the street. Inside, some features are almost breathtaking, the walls adorned with oil paintings and antique furniture dotted around the buildings as if on show. Its Spanish architecture, originally built as a hotel by oil baron Henry Flagler, is now one of the most attractive academic institutions in the state.

McCabe looked relieved as he slid off the back of the Harley. He was breathless and felt as if he'd run the journey instead of being a passenger on a motorcycle. He pulled off his helmet and took a grateful mouthful of air.

Tracy had already taken off hers, shook her long hair back into some sort of shape and was making for the stairwell of the main building.

'What are we doing here?' he asked, still panting as he careered after her.

'I've someone to meet. You can come along with me; heaven knows if you shut-up for a few minutes you might learn something.'

Another barb to ignore, thought McCabe. He said nothing.

The corridors were a cross between those of an old manor house and the passageways of an ancient castle. This was no new-build and it had been maintained well. 'It used to be a hotel, or at least parts of it built by Flagler the oilman,' she said, as if she were a tour guide. 'In the eighteen hundreds, I think. Now the students enjoy the antique furniture and the valuable artwork. What neat backdrop this is, eh?'

They moved through several doorways, at least half a dozen small arches then up two more flights of stairs.

At last, Tracy the tireless tour guide, stopped outside a studded doorway shaped like the entrance to a small church. The iron door handle creaked as she turned it, as did the door when it opened. 'Professor?' she enquired, quietly. She pushed the door open further to reveal an office that could only have belonged to an academic. Piles of papers and books were stacked in no obvious order. The only concession to the modern world was a desktop computer.

'Tracy,' said a voice from a white-haired figure behind the computer. 'Tracy,' he repeated. 'Always a pleasure; come in, come in. I got your text,' he said as he waved the latest iphone. 'It is very interesting, very interesting.'

Chapter 18

Daytona Beach, Florida

As a cub reporter, he'd always thought it fun to people-watch; trying to match someone's appearance to their occupation. The success rate varied but McCabe remembered at one press conference when he'd confidently classified an untidy dishevelled youth as a member of a local punk band who'd lost his way and arrived at the wrong place. At the end of the event the youth was presented with a prize for his outstanding advances in Nuclear Physics research at a top London university. That day taught him a lesson.

However, the white haired professor seated behind the desk, stacked with books and piles of papers, wasn't far from McCabe's image of the cloistered academic. But Professor Mervin Collins, like the scruffy youth of years ago, had his contradictions. He was not a man one would expect to be an enthusiast of the modern world but would be more comfortable steeped in his old ways; not so.

'I love this technology,' he explained to Tracy. 'It has made my research so much easier.'

She moved behind his desk and sat beside him, as if she was about to perform a duet with him on a piano.

He pointed to the computer and ran his right index finger down a row of numbers on the screen. 'When I got your text, I ran a few pieces of software which were sent to me by one of my ex-students.' He laughed. 'Such a naughty boy that student, you know,' he said as he continued to enjoy the memory. 'Straight A's in everything.' He continued to chuckle. 'He developed this software for the Coast Guard.'

'Wouldn't that be classified?' asked McCabe.

Garrison gave him one of her melting looks.

McCabe shrugged his shoulders in his defence.

The professor sensed his awkwardness. 'Tracy, also one of my ex-students, is a little rough about some edges. Do forgive her approach. She means well, is a bright kid and very mischievous,' he said, as if writing her school report. He roared with laughter again. 'And where are her manners? She didn't even introduce us, although she did send me your biog.' He continued to study the figures on the screen. 'I was impressed by what I read, Mr. McCabe. You seem to have irritated a few political power brokers in your day.' He rocked a little in his chair, almost like an excited child. 'Well done! I bet that was fun. I've fantasised about doing something like that one day. Sadly, it'll only be in my dreams.'

They all joined in his laughter.

'But don't worry. I also wear another hat. We're not breaking the law. I've got the appropriate security clearance. The government calls me from time to time. I suspect they're monitoring some of the things we are.'

McCabe didn't quite follow.

Garrison produced her phone, brought up the text she'd downloaded from the blog publisher.

The professor scrolled through the text. He shook his head. 'The woman who wrote the blog says there was another boat not far from where she saw the yacht.' He turned to Garrison. 'That doesn't tell us anything, does it?'

McCabe felt confident that someone would eventually explain what was going on. He decided to take the initiative. 'What are you looking for?' he asked, almost timidly.

The professor gave another of his chuckles. 'Ah, she didn't explain that to you either. She is a naughty girl,' he said looking straight at Garrison again.

McCabe looked grateful for the rescue.

'Research is a bit like journalism, Mr. McCabe. You don't know what you'll find. Invariably you don't know what you're looking for,' explained the professor, now holding McCabe in his gaze. He turned to the girl. 'I'll let her brief you in detail but essentially we've been monitoring the movement of boats in and out of Florida.'

'Why?'

The professor pressed a key on Garrison's mobile and watched as the data transferred to the computer screen. 'I maybe an old academic from a different generation but I'm always amazed by today's technology. I'm ecstatic about it all.' He inspected the text which had appeared on the screen then typed in a few instructions on his keyboard. 'I'll put in the coordinates of the vessels and see what comes up.'

'That's what the software you mentioned is meant to do?'

The professor didn't answer for a moment. He finished inspecting the data. 'Yes, supposedly,' said the professor, as another display appeared on the screen.

McCabe moved closer to the machine. The rows of numbers didn't tell him anything.

The professor sensed McCabe was struggling. 'Forgive me. I guess, I'd better explain.' He stood up, walked across the room to a small white board and picked up a pointer. 'Another piece of technology; it's great no chalk or dusters.' He had another chuckle. 'I research and teach mathematics, specialising in a subject called *Operational Research*. It goes by a few names but journalists have used a version of it to generate stories.'

McCabe shook his head. 'I'm a wordsmith, professor. Make it simple.'

The jovial professor had another laugh. He evidently enjoyed his work. He gestured towards Garrison. 'Tracy came to our summer school and decided to do a project on the movement of yachts in and out of some small ports in Florida.'

'You discovered something interesting?' quizzed McCabe.

The professor leaned forward and tapped the computer. He explained how it was only meant as an academic exercise but soon it was evident that there was a definable pattern. Some vessels were more active than others, in excess of what would be considered normal. 'We identified a couple of vessels that were of particular interest.'

'So, what did you find out?'

The professor laughed out loud again. 'Found out? Absolutely nothing apart from sailing patterns.'

McCabe looked disappointed.

Again the professor was very astute. He sensed McCabe still looked muddled. 'I'm a mathematician Mr.McCabe, not a detective. After our initial findings, I wrote a paper for a conference about sailing patterns. It wasn't long before the Coast Guard were on the phone.'

'Their interest is obvious, which I have to admit, until now had escaped me; smuggling,' commented McCabe.

'Exactly,' said the professor. 'But Tracy guessed that this same technique could be used to follow the sailing patterns of particular boats, tapping into our data on wind, currents, tides, time of day; all that stuff.'

Tracy who had been standing on the other side of the professor pointed to the numbers of the screen. 'I was hoping the professor could help me find out where *The Georgia* had been.'

Collins shook his head. 'I don't think so; not enough data. But I think we can confirm from the details in the blog you acquired that the sighting was *The Georgia*. I suspect my friends in the Coast Guard know a lot more about that boat than we do. Perhaps they'll share it with us?' He laughed aloud again. 'I doubt that! But I'm curious. What's your interest in this Mr.McCabe? If it's smuggling, you've come to the right part of the country.'

McCabe had been asking himself the same question. There was a story here; of that he was sure. All the indicators suggested it was a good one. But what was it? Tracy's tale was of a smuggling operation gone wrong. Somehow he felt it was much more. There was nothing in Meyer's houseboat that gave any clue to what he'd been doing. Certainly he had lived an adventurous life and had flirted with danger as a profession but a decorated ex-navy hero, now turned smuggler, didn't make any sense.

Chapter 19

Daytona Beach, Florida

McCabe had told Tracy nothing, although she'd read the article he'd written on Meyer's arrival aboard the drifting yacht. She'd then guessed his interest. It was unlikely she'd briefed the Flagler professor.

He made his own overtures.

'The man who was murdered was a neighbour of mine in DC. That's my interest,' McCabe said eventually. It wasn't a lie but it wasn't the entire picture either. What that canvas looked like, he didn't know himself. But his instincts told him that the story had to be much bigger than a tale of a man who'd got into bad company, jettisoned his previous life, became a smuggler and then it all went bad. He didn't buy it.

Clearly the clue was Meyer himself. Was it danger or adventure that stimulated this naval hero or something less obvious? Within that list of possible motives was the key to this story.

'So, you're interested in the human angle, Mr. McCabe?' the professor asked.

'Yes, sort of,' McCabe answered with a little hesitation. The truth was he didn't know what aspect would interest him but instinctively he could tell the amiable academic sensed his uncertainty. 'That's my interest and perhaps a little more. With respect professor, statistics don't excite me. People and their behaviour do,' McCabe said, quite emphatically.

Collins understood. He was no fool. 'The story behind the story,' quizzed the academic. 'Any particular aspect?'

McCabe sensed he was being tested or did he always feel that in the presence of a teacher, a throwback from his unsuccessful schooldays? It was too long ago to remember. Perhaps academics lived in a different world to him? It wasn't a world of which he had much experience.

'You feel uncomfortable with the academic mind, Mr. McCabe?' Collins asked. 'But there is something else gnawing at you, about the Meyer case. Am I right?'

McCabe smiled at the professor's astute observations.

'Professor, you're an expert on government, are you not?'

Collins nodded. 'Yes, I teach and research the subject; American and European. What particular aspect interests you then?'

McCabe hesitated for a moment. 'Organised crime,' he said emphatically.

Tracy, who'd been focused on the computer output, turned her attention to McCabe.

'I see,' said Collins. 'Any particular culture?'

'Russian.'

Tracy looked surprised. This was all news to her.

'You're right, I'm not an academic,' conceded McCabe. 'But I did read an article by some professor on the rise of organised crime and the disintegration of the Soviet Union. The ideas impressed me. They also frightened me.'

Collins gave out one of his signature chuckles. 'There's been a lot written about the subject, some good, some rubbish, even by academics. Crime has always been with us. In many countries around the world, where social changes take place, sometimes when chaos reigns, it's a feeding ground for crime and corruption where wealth and power are the prizes to be fought over,' he replied as if giving a lecture. He'd delivered that one before, thought McCabe.

McCabe enjoyed the eloquence but he wanted more. 'I was particularly interested in the Soviets.'

'Why?'

'I've been thinking about this incident in St. Augustine and there seemed to be certain similarities.' It had been a theory running around in his mind without any substance. Police Chief Fischer had some suspicions. He'd asked whether Meyer had any Russian friends. He must have discovered something. That wasn't much to go on.

'Crime is the same the whole world over,' continued the professor. 'It's usually motivated by greed or lust. Is there any other kind? You haven't answered me. Why the Soviets?'

McCabe shook his head. 'As we discussed earlier, I'm groping, I'm looking for the clue, just like you said, the one that will lead me to the solution.'

'But someone or something must have pointed you in that direction, surely?'

McCabe shrugged. There was nothing that didn't sound banal.

The professor seemed to answer his own question. 'When the Soviet state disintegrated there were all sorts of factions running for cover. There was a lack of cohesion, social order, political infrastructure, hierarchy and an abundance of opportunity to make money, legitimate or not. There were already criminal gangs operating in the country, manned by career criminals and ex-servicemen, out to sell their combat skills....'

'And killing skills,' interjected McCabe.

'But it's a very confused picture. For a while there was a blurred line between the powers that ran the state and those in the underworld, at least some academics thought so.'

'And now?'

'Some people are still debating that issue.'

'What's your take on it?' asked McCabe, as he pulled out his notebook and scribbled a few lines. 'Do excuse me professor; an aide memoire.'

The professor was now in full flight. 'Some career criminals came from the Gulags, some are veterans with nothing but their soldiering skills to sell, others were already on the streets making a living in a society in chaos.'

McCabe checked his notebook for something. He read a line or two from one of the pages. 'For me, the interesting part of the article I read was their activities abroad. They're now in the export business. Spain and the UK have had particular problems, the article stated.'

The professor said nothing for a moment but stared at McCabe. He then began to speak quietly, as if he was sharing a confidence. 'So now it's the USA? Is that your contention?'

McCabe nodded. 'I've seen ritual executions before. One shot in the head; the work of a professional marksman, not a crime of passion.'

'You're still talking about the dead man on the boat?'

'Yes,' said McCabe unequivocally.

'But we've had organised crime, as you call it, since the days of Al Capone, if not before. Why the Russians?' argued the professor.

'Smuggling and people trafficking; I'd have thought this part of the world would have been perfect for that kind of activity.'

'Have you spoken to the police about this THEORY of yours?' asked Collins, emphasising the word.

McCabe looked a little uncomfortable, if not embarrassed. 'It's not a theory,' he said quietly. 'It's just a thought I had,' he lied, throwing the word back at the professor.

Collins smiled and stood up. 'Could be; as I said, if you want to find smugglers you've come to the right part of the state.'

McCabe took the cue and made for the door, still uncertain whether his ideas had made any sense.

The professor hadn't dismissed them outright. 'You could be right, Mr. McCabe. I wish you all the best in your story. I enjoyed our chat but, I'm afraid, I have a lecture to give. But let me leave with one thought. The criminal element, whatever you like to call it, is perhaps only part of the equation. If you're right, be careful. These guys play hardball. That's code for notoriously ruthless.'

Chapter 20

Washington, DC

Dwight Sanchez, feeling a little worse for another lunchtime indulgence, couldn't get his front door lock and key to coordinate. He staggered back slightly, checked that he had made the right selection and tried the lock again. This time the two engaged and he heard the familiar click as the door gave way. He picked up the mail from the doormat, usually slipped through his letterbox by his neighbour, who'd got it from the rack at the gate to the compound. It was a friendly gesture, meant to prevent a predictable pile-up of unclaimed mail. He felt comfortable there. It was his home.

Sanchez felt his career was well and truly stalled, if not over. He'd been in National Security, in some form or other, since he'd left college and like everyone else in his year, he was full of ambitions and noble goals. He wasn't the type who could easily operate in the field. So his role was to be counted among the ranks of the intelligence gathering youths whose spark energised the bottom rungs of the CIA. In time, the job was like that of any researcher at a university or institute. He'd trawl academic papers, quality newspapers – foreign and domestic - and earmark anything that would add to the Agency's databank of intelligence.

But the political masters on Capitol Hill had decided, in the wake of nine-eleven and the fear of further attacks, to coordinate their efforts under the umbrella of Homeland Security. The Agency still had its identity but he felt it had lost some clout. Perhaps it was him. He had to admit that his marriage breakup and subsequently the drink issue had played their parts in his poor performance. It hadn't gone unnoticed. He wasn't obviously demoted but his projects appeared to be of diminishing importance. His personal and professional life was faltering, if not spiralling out of control.

At least the journalist he'd met, a few days earlier, found his insight useful. Meeting the journalist gave a much-needed boost to his self-confidence and meant his experience still had some currency. Undoubtedly, his employer would take a dim view of his extramural activities.

In retrospect perhaps talking to a journalist wasn't the smartest of moves. He'd been too casual, if not reckless, in his hint at the conflicts within the Agency. But he'd seen the signs; conversations suddenly lowered when he passed or dropped to a whisper. He'd often wondered if he'd made any enemies?

Too many in the organisation preferred the old ways when their authority was free from the prying eyes of their political overlords. He knew such insurgency could spell danger; it was too easy for some to make their own rules. He had some ideas about dissent groups but hadn't elaborated to the journalist over lunch. But McCabe was no fool and as his reputation suggested, he only needed to be put in the direction of the fox to get the scent. Care was required.

He staggered unsteadily into his kitchen. He had no idea what force hit him and never heard a sound as a right-hand chopped down onto the back of his neck. The style was professional, immediate and silent. He was dead before he hit the tiled floor.

The residents in this quiet neighbourhood of DC rarely noticed any comings and goings. The workmen in overalls who left one of the houses carrying what looked like the rolled up remains of a carpet were almost invisible in this suburb.

The body of Dwight Sanchez would never be found.

That was the plan. But the workmen's exit was clumsy. By the time they'd got to their truck, parked a few yards from the compound, the police had received at least three phone calls. Within half an hour the normal homicide DC police had been relieved of any investigative responsibilities and the government security agencies had elbowed them aside.

By then the genie was well and truly out of the bottle.

Chapter 21

St. Augustine, Florida

Locked in her thoughts, Darlene Shannon didn't notice the two people leaving Flagler College, opposite where she was having coffee. The fuzzy photo she'd been sent with the biography of McCabe was a few years old and barely flattering. Had the snap been clearer, she probably still wouldn't have responded. Her thoughts were elsewhere.

The death of Meyer seemed to have dominated every waking hour in recent days, and some of the nights too. Before he turned up as a corpse on a drifting stolen boat, he was scheduled to sail on the luxury liner. That had been the plan. So what went wrong?

So far, one dead was the score; at least that was her reading. She might soon add one missing to that count; Irina Lukin. The link between the two, and that was barely tenuous, was the *Orient Atlantic*.

She pulled up a file on her tablet and scanned the text carefully. It read: *May James, real name Irina Lukin, American of Russian descent.* The remainder of the file made interesting, if not predictable, reading. She'd waited table for a few years after high school in her home town of Baltimore. Supposedly, her grandfather had been a Russian sailor who had married an American on arrival in the US, jumped ship and so the family was born. Grandfather was last seen alive in a poker game in a less than salubrious, dangerous and seedy part of the waterfront. Two days later he was found floating, face down in the harbour, his only ID a photograph of his family with an address on the back. Her grandmother soon found herself alone bringing up three children in that rundown part of the city.

Not surprisingly, Irina had started life on a low social rung. Barely out of her teens with no qualifications and even less prospects, she reinvented herself as May James, entertainer, in certain quarters the street-speak for hooker. She'd graduated from the back alleys of Baltimore to the big time, 'entertaining' rich male clients on board luxury liners which sailed from Florida. She lived well for services rendered but her clientele were dangerous people.

Shannon scrolled through the file. She wanted to find some sympathy for the girl who'd been short-changed all her life but it was hard for her and didn't come naturally.

Life hadn't handed her anything. Everything she'd got she'd damn well earned and it had hardened her; that she knew only too well. Without a cutting edge, that ruthless focus, she knew she was going nowhere. She was not to be a casualty, considered over-ambitious and lacking in the mettle to get the job done. Nor was she going to be a statistic, a loser laughed about by her male colleagues in the club bar.

So was Lukin a casualty before she'd even been recruited? Aboard the *Orient Atlantic* she and Meyer had become close. Whether they were lovers she didn't know, nor cared. Perhaps he'd been a client of hers at the beginning? That didn't matter either. How he tackled his assignment was of little interest. His job was simple; get someone who knew the ship and its players. Whatever method he used to cement their relationship was his choice; results were Shannon's only focus.

Undoubtedly, the ship was a conduit for a myriad of illegal activities and cargo but she could prove nothing. She guessed there was much more. What was the well-guarded secret, the one that Meyer was to discover and the one he paid for with his life?

Shannon sat in her car, pulled up the email on her tablet and checked the address on screen twice before pushing the door open. The apartment block was dowdy and in a less fashionable part of town, a poor neighbourhood outside St. Augustine, home to rows of cheap food outlets, low-grade motels and shoddy stores.

Irina Lukin didn't answer to the first two rings of the doorbell on the ground-floor apartment. When she did, it was cautious. The door opened slightly, as she peered at the visitor.

Shannon's badge was enough for the door to open slightly. But it took a lot of persuasion before any further progress was made. Meyer's name and Shannon's revulsion at his death released the door further.

Lukin, looking distressed, led the way into the lounge and sat on the sofa.

'They killed him like they've killed others,' she said, without preamble, her hands visibly shaking. She fumbled her way through opening a packet of cigarettes, clumsily extracted one and put one in her mouth. She had difficulty lighting it as she continued to tremble. 'They'll kill me too.'

Shannon took the lighter from her, clicked it and moved the flame slowly towards her. 'You need to tell me what happened. I can protect you.'

Lukin glared at her. 'You've no idea who you're playing with here, no fucking idea. Protect me, my ass? Is that what you said to Harry? Look at him now.'

Shannon stood still, concerned the slightest move might disturb the equilibrium. 'Perhaps you could tell me what happened; share that with me?' she asked quietly.

Lukin stared straight ahead sucking heavily on the cigarette and then slowly exhaling. She was still trembling as she gripped her skirt tightly with her free hand. 'They'll get us all,' she said quietly. 'You know what I mean? Get us all.'

Shannon came closer and sat beside her. She could see the dark shadows under Lukin's eyes.

The rest of the girl's face looked drawn and strained, as if she hadn't slept for days.

'I told him not to take the risk,' she said shaking her head. 'I told him but he wouldn't listen.'

Shannon moved even closer and stretched out to hold the hand gripping the skirt. It felt cold, clammy and was still trembling. 'What risk?'

Shannon felt awkward but she had to press. Anything she would say to comfort her was going to sound trite if not patronising. She took the cigarette from her and stubbed it out in the ashtray.

'I think you need some sleep. I'll stay with you while you get some rest.'

'I don't need any rest,' Lukin snapped at her then smiled in apology. 'Sorry, my nerves are a bit shattered. I've got something to take; in the kitchen cabinet.' She made to get up but sank back into her chair. She looked exhausted.

Lukin was in a bad way and she needed expert medical help. 'You stay where you are,' said Shannon and walked quickly across the lounge and into the kitchen. Before she opened the cabinet she had a feeling that she'd find nothing and equally certain when she raced back to the lounge it would be empty.

The door to the apartment was open. She could hear the car tyres screech as they spun to get traction as it sped down the driveway. 'Fuck,' she screamed as loud as she could. As the sound echoed in the small room she suddenly realised the extent of her outburst. She sat for a moment scanning the room for some clue that might make this fiasco worthwhile. A rummage through all the drawers in the room, the bedroom and the kitchen produced nothing. One framed photograph of a handsome man in his thirties was mounted on a small bookcase. She opened the frame and examined the back of the photo; nothing.

Chapter 22

Washington, DC

A world away from Florida, Senator Viktor Segal, Democrat from Virginia, slowly pulled his Nissan up to the security gate, gave the guard his customary wave, waited until the barrier lifted then drove into his usual space at the far end of the Senate parking lot.

It was a crisp morning. He could see the splendour of Union Station in the distance and behind him the majestic architecture of the dome over Congress. He quickly locked the car, went through the routine tedium of the security checks as he entered the main Senate building and within five minutes had weaved his way via the numerous corridors to his office. The large doors to his outer office were open and his two secretaries were hard at work. He looked at his watch. They'd probably been there for an hour or so. He had a slight pang of guilt but he knew that would pass.

He pointed to the coffee machine as he made his way through towards the inner office. One of his secretaries, a young man of breathtaking efficiency, had already filled up a cup and had placed it on the desk. Segal smiled in appreciation then sank into his leather chair. A copy of the Washington Post, the New York Times and the Wall Street Journal were in a pile on the right-hand side of the desk. He smiled again at the efficiency. A stack of correspondence, already sliced open, lay in the middle of the desk. He lifted them to one side as he began to drink his coffee. Beneath the pile was a medium-sized white envelope. On inspection he saw it hadn't been open. He shrugged then opened it. His face lost its smile as he pulled out a brochure. He called through to the outer office. 'Jason, do you have a moment?'

The young man, Jason Miller, was at the desk in seconds. 'Where did this come from,' Segal asked standing in front of his desk and waving the envelope. He looked distraught. 'It was on my desk below the pile of mail.'

The young man took it, inspected the blank front cover, turned it over then handed it back. 'I thought you'd left it there yourself, sir. That's why it's not opened.'

'So, it was already there when you came in with the morning mail?'

'Yes; it was on your desk,' Miller said slowly.

'Was the office locked when you arrived?'

The young man didn't hesitate. 'I was first to arrive. It was locked, as usual. The cleaners are given access to clean the carpets and empty the rubbish.' He stopped for a moment and looked at the untidy desk. 'In the outer office, sir, we make it a policy not to leave things on desks. We lock everything away.' It sounded like a reprimand.

'I didn't leave that envelope,' the congressman snapped. He walked back to his chair and stared at the envelope lying on his desk. His ruddy facial colour which had been prominent ten minutes before had suddenly dissipated and in its place was an anaemic drawn look. He appeared in shock and confused. He dismissed the young man with a wave from the back of his right hand. 'Ok. I'll deal with it.'

He sunk even deeper into the chair. How could he deal with this? He wasn't sure what it meant. Was the sender telling him something? Was getting into his office a demonstration of how easy it was to gain access to him? Was the burglar saying that next time he wouldn't be delivering an envelope but something more sinister, more fatal?

Segal pulled out the contents of the envelope again and laid it flat on the desk. He shook his head several times and let out a sigh, a mixture of anxiety and fear. He pulled open his desk, brought out a small leather notebook, selected a section separated by a red marker, ran his finger down the listing and stopped. His finger seemed to waiver over the name and number. He lifted up his cell phone, began to dial the number then stopped. He reached for the security of his office phone. He pressed the button for a direct outside line and dialled the number. He was about to hang up when a voice-mail answer system kicked in. He hung up immediately. His mouth was now dry and his hands a little moist. He sighed again as he looked at the content he'd spread on the desk. Prominent on the brochure-cover was a photo of the *Orient Atlantic.*

Chapter 23

St. Augustine, Florida

CNN flickered in the background as McCabe made himself a jug of martini in his hotel room. It was hardly a health kick he was on but the light cocktail was more moderate than a double scotch. He was trying to be a good boy, at least for a week or two. It happened once a year after he'd read some alarmist article. He knew it was probably written by some hack under pressure from his editor to write something about health. But he'd fallen for it again. He knew, if he was being honest, that his whisky bottle didn't take long in emptying. So, inevitably every so often he'd get a health scare. Such was the plight of the man who lived alone; so the health soothsayers predicted, doom-merchants all.

He vaguely heard the television reporter giving his spiel in the background. A word caught his ear. It sounded like '*Sanchez*'. He turned his attention to the channel, grabbed the remote and pressed the volume control. '*Dwight Sanchez lived in this apartment block,*' said the reporter turning towards the building to his side. '*According to neighbours, he was quiet, unassuming and kept himself to himself.*'

McCabe looked disturbed. 'Forget the fucking clichés, tell me what happened,' he shouted at the screen.

It was the end of the TV report.

McCabe channel hopped looking for more; nothing. He threw the remote on sofa, raced to his desk and fired up his laptop. One search on the name was enough. The text flew onto the screen from a Washington-based news website.

Dwight Sanchez, a government employee, was discovered murdered in his home in DC today. The details are few but Sanchez, a researcher for an undisclosed government department, was believed killed yesterday. Neighbours noticed two men leaving the house in Takoma Park late last night carrying something suspicious and alerted the police. When the police arrived they found it was a body which they believe will prove to be Dwight Sanchez.

McCabe was stunned. He took a mouthful of martini as he slumped onto the sofa and gazed back at the television looking for an update. He was trying to get his thoughts in order, to remember his last meeting with Sanchez, what he had said to him, what he recalled from the conversation and above all what he may have missed. Immediately, he delved into the inside pocket of his coat carelessly thrown across a chair. He hadn't taken too many notes in the Sanchez meeting but he took a few. He flipped through the pages to remind him of the conversation. There was nothing he could see.

It was easy to spring to conclusions but there was nothing to indicate that the murder and their meeting were in any way connected. McCabe flipped through the pages again. Certainly, Sanchez had hinted to look behind the obvious storyline. But he was drunk and by virtue of his background, innocently described as a researcher for a government department, he'd a tendency to see shadows in too many places. He was neurotic and unstable. But he did know his business. That's why he was a good source. It could have been Sanchez's way of saying he was still a player, was still important. Perhaps it was more than pretence.

There were always limitations on the value of information proffered by any source. Few were accurate accounts. They'd been embellished one way or another. It was human nature and most sources had an axe to grind, some angle which gave their ideas more importance. The required talent was knowing what was valuable, what had been given a jaundiced top spin and what was complete rubbish, without being too cynical. Was there something in the notes he'd missed that was meant to caution McCabe? Had Sanchez been aware of a threat to his life and said so, in some disguised way? Did he hint at something and McCabe had missed it? Perhaps Sanchez had told him more than he'd wanted. He certainly had enough alcohol to loosen his tongue. Or was he killed for what he hadn't told McCabe but what his killers thought he had? Of course it could be just one of the senseless murders that took place in the American capital every day; violence without purpose or motive.

He'd been staring at the television for all of ten minutes.

A knock on the door, almost in unison with the telephone ringing, woke him from the trance. He was nearer the handset than the door; two steps and he had it. 'McCabe,' he answered briskly.

'This is the front desk. There is a gentleman to see you sir. I'm sorry but he wouldn't wait. He's on his way up.'

McCabe had almost forgotten about the martini. He finished it as he dropped the phone on the cradle. The cocktail was a little weak. He sucked the olive on the stick, as he made for the door. It needed more gin; definitely more gin. He should have stuck to scotch. This health fad was going to be short-lived. The impatient knocker banged on the door again. One more stride and he had the door open.

Chief Fischer didn't look in the least bit apologetic for the intrusion. He walked assertively passed McCabe into the room.

'Do come in,' said McCabe, gesturing with an open hand. 'Make yourself at home, Chief.' He was hoping the sarcasm didn't go unnoticed.

The policeman walked to the end of the room, checked the dressing area and had a quick look through the open door of the bathroom.

'We are alone, Chief,' assured McCabe. 'Can I offer you a martini?'

Fischer sat on a chair by the table. 'I think we should have a chat.'

McCabe's first reaction was that he was there because of the death of Sanchez. But there was no way the policeman had any knowledge of that connection. Surely, they had finished the Meyer interview? He was trying to fathom why he was there.

'I thought we had exhausted our conversation,' said McCabe quickly. 'It wasn't too inspiring, as far as I can recall,' he

continued then sampled another of his martini-jug again. He looked at the cocktail stick floating in the drink. 'I made loads,' he added pointing to the jug on top of the fridge. 'Don't feel obliged; it wasn't too successful. It definitely needs more gin.'
Fischer ignored the offer. 'This is not a social call,' he said bluntly. 'I thought I'd prevent another one of your theatrical outbursts, accusing us of dragging you somewhere without your consent.'

'As if I would?' commented McCabe in an attempt to be humorous. It fell flat.

The Police Chief was not amused.

'Sorry,' apologised McCabe immediately. 'What can I do for you?'

Fischer looked determined, as if a man on a mission. 'Do you know a girl called May James?'

It wasn't the question McCabe was expecting. 'No; I've never heard of her. Should I?'

Fischer sighed a little, as he shuffled on his chair.

McCabe detected impatience, if not frustration.

'It would be helpful if you let me ask the questions,' said the policeman, showing his irritation.

'OK'. McCabe couldn't suppress a slight smile. He liked the policeman's directness.

'She was born Irina Lukin.'

'Russian?'

'American of Russian descent.'

McCabe looked puzzled. Trying to read Fischer had been a challenge. The policeman would have made a great poker player, he thought; a face which betrayed nothing and showed not the slightest emotion. 'Why would I know this girl?' Fischer stared at him again. 'I thought I'd told you about the questions,' he said. 'Remember; I ask them, you answer.'
McCabe was unhappy with the tone. The little humour that there was, had gone out of the exchange. 'Look, you come waltzing in here asking me obscure questions about someone I've never heard of and I'm not supposed to ask why?' McCabe had raised his voice unintentionally. But he was having difficulty suppressing his annoyance.

The policeman looked as if he accepted the reasoning. 'I will have a small martini,' he said with perfect timing; a professional diversion.

McCabe smiled and poured them both a drink. 'It's not the greatest sample but I think it'll help the two of us a little.

'She was a girlfriend of Harry Meyer,' said Fischer as he took the glass.

'And your interest in her is what?'

Fischer seemed to be debating something. Clearly too much disclosure was uncomfortable for him too.

McCabe sympathised. They were singing from the same song sheet.

'Have you ever heard of a cruise ship called the *Orient Atlantic*?'

The question took McCabe aback. His face said so. Before he could answer the policeman had answered his own question. I know you have; I spoke to the same agent you did.'

McCabe wasn't sure how to respond now. He was as uncomfortable disclosing too much information with the police as he was with the press.

But Fischer looked as if he had most of the cards. He pulled out his cell phone and pressed a button. He kept looking straight ahead, almost through McCabe, as he began to speak into his handset. He turned away, murmured a few sentences. 'But she's OK?' he asked, as he turned back. He appeared quite insistent. McCabe's eyebrows pulled together. His confusion was evident. He hadn't got the thread yet.

'A curious coincidence, don't you think?' asked the policeman. 'We were on our way to interview her. But before we could get to her, someone else did?'

'Someone else did?' repeated McCabe. 'Someone else did what?'

Again, the policeman was struggling against saying too much. 'Her car was sideswiped on the freeway outside St. Augustine.' He watched the journalist closely for a reaction.

'Is she OK?' McCabe asked sounding genuinely concerned.

'She made it,' said the policeman softly. 'But only just.'

Chapter 24

St. Augustine, Florida

The face of the pale figure in the bed through the glass wall, immersed in a helix of tubes and wires, was difficult to identify. McCabe stared through the glass trying to determine whether any of what little was visible was recognisable at all. Bruises, cuts and blood dotted the face of the patient lying in the bed about twelve feet away.

Irina Lukin, car crash victim, was on a life-support system, fighting to survive.

Chief Fischer reluctantly shared the viewing spot. 'I don't know what you're doing here, McCabe,' he said walking towards the door of the patient's room. 'As you can see,' he continued nodding towards the two policemen flanking the doorway. 'There will be no interviews.'

McCabe looked uneasy. He knew the policeman wasn't a man who responded easily to persuasion. 'Chief,' he started quietly keeping an eye on the girl. 'I think we're after the same thing.'

'And what would that be?'

'The truth,' fired McCabe, although of old he knew there was no such absolute. 'As near as we can,' he added softly. 'Not always easy to determine.'

'You still haven't answered my question.'

'Was there a question?'

Fischer looked irritated. It wasn't the best of responses.

McCabe detected the tension. 'I'm working on a story, Chief. You know my interest. You said she was Meyer's girlfriend.' The description sounded vague at best, at worse it sounded stupid.

Fischer still looked annoyed. 'You mean he was sleeping with her?'

'I have no idea what personal relationship they had. I care even less.' That answer sounded cynical. 'I'm working on a story; you're on the same case. We have some common ground.'

Fischer, for the moment, looked as if he was considering. 'What are you offering?'

McCabe walked to the end of the corridor, pulled out his notebook, flipped through a few pages and looked back at the policeman staring after him. He didn't have much to trade, except Sanchez. But that source was now dead and at this stage would add nothing to the equation. There was too much guesswork and not enough facts.

He didn't know whether the death of Sanchez had anything to do with his story or the policeman's investigation. Perhaps the Mexican and Meyer were just victims of mindless violence, all too commonplace? Perhaps both were coincidences, whose tragic circumstances were unrelated?

But he couldn't talk about Sanchez. The policeman would want to know who he was, what his connection was to the tale and ask a thousand questions, the majority to which McCabe had no answer. It would be way too convoluted to attempt to explain.

McCabe closed the notebook. He had nothing to trade.

Fischer had turned back and was now staring through the glass again.

McCabe coughed slightly, caught the policeman's attention, gave him a parting nod and walked to the exit.

Chapter 25

Washington, DC

Senator Segal parked his car in the street about a block from his small townhouse in Georgetown, northwest Washington. He was still disturbed. The contents of the blank envelope waiting on his desk to greet him that morning had haunted him all day. He'd stared at the brochure of the *Atlantic Orient* for more than half an hour, trying to determine its meaning, the motive of the person who sent it and what was wanted. Whoever had delivered it had an agenda. It was meant to frighten him as was the content. The picture of the cruise ship was significant.

He pulled the offending envelope from a leather case and extracted the brochure. Perhaps it was harmless, a travel brochure that had been sent to all the congressmen. It would be a good marketing ploy. Somehow he wasn't satisfied with that theory. Also, with little effort, someone had broken into his office. That was unnerving in itself. His security had been well breached. He'd checked all his filing cabinets, to see if anything was missing. They were all locked. He'd inspected the contents. Everything appeared to be intact. The delivery of the brochure carried a deliberate message. He didn't know what it was but it scared him.

His house was unusually silent as he closed the front door. He threw his keys on the small table. His wife was out and would probably not return until late in the evening. The drinks cabinet beckoned. It was easier to indulge when his wife was away. He poured a large gin with just a splash of tonic, a slice of lemon and a handful of ice. He could feel himself relaxing as he slid into one of the armchairs beside the fireplace and took a mouthful of the drink. He hadn't noticed the figure in the recess at the end of the bookcase.

It wasn't long before it moved out the shadows and made its presence known. It was there to ensure that the envelope had been delivered, its content read and its message understood. The visit was meant to upset the senator even more.

It wasn't until well after midnight that the emergency services received a call from an upset householder in Georgetown. She tried to explain, in near hysteria, that she'd returned home to find the body of her husband lying on the lounge floor. Only at the last minute, in her panic, did she mention that her husband was a US Senator.

Jason Miller watched from the sidewalk as the medics wheeled out their patient on a trolley. Not surprisingly, the flashing lights of the ambulance had attracted several from the neighbourhood. Some had known the senator while others were just plain nosey.

The young man barely caught a glimpse of the face underneath the oxygen mask. Given the senator had suffered a heart attack and had collapsed he still had some colour in his face. At least that was the diagnosis of the gossipmongers who crowded around the Georgetown townhouse. Some claimed it was mild, others that it was critical. There were some who predicted the congressman was at death's door. The only real truth was that he was in a bad way and had been found by his wife on her return from a night out.

Jason Miller slid past the crowd blocking the stairs and managed to get halfway to the front door without being stopped by the determined forearm of a uniformed patrolman. The young man showed his Senate Staffer security badge, explained who he was and climbed the last few steps to the front door.

He'd been concerned at the distressed state of the senator when he'd left for home earlier in the day. An attack brought on by anxiety now didn't surprise him, although he had no clue to the cause. Through the open door, he could see the senator's wife sitting on the sofa in the middle of the lounge.

She caught sight of him and signalled.

He walked past the policeman and joined her on the sofa. 'I'm speechless. I was concerned about him and decided to bring over these papers which arrived after he left,' he said lifting up the pile he'd been holding under an arm.

'You were concerned?' She sounded worried.

Miller looked at the open door.

'Please close the door,' she called to the policeman. 'I'll be following the ambulance shortly.'

When the door closed, she turned back to Miller. 'Concerned? About what?'

Miller smiled nervously. He didn't want to be an alarmist but it was clear the senator had been troubled. They'd been together for several years and he'd become familiar with his moods and temperament. Normally not a man who would be easily unsettled, something had caused him distress. Judging by the senator's earlier questions, the catalyst was the blank white enveloped he'd been waving. Had the content been what caused the disquiet?

The congressman had been fairly buoyant when he'd arrived that morning. In less than a minute his mood had changed to one of anxiety and unease. In between something had happened. The plain white envelope he was waving looked the likely culprit.

The young man ignored her question. 'Tell me, what happened?' he asked quickly.

Her answer sounded shrill, as if she too was in shock. 'I'd been out most of the evening. When I came in, I found him on the carpet. He didn't look as if he was breathing,' she recalled, holding her hands together tightly. 'I think I might have panicked. I phoned emergency immediately. But I don't think I was too clear. They might have got here earlier had I .....,' she didn't finish; the sentence faded away. She was obviously distraught and blamed herself for the outcome.

He leaned across and touched her hands.

As she rose and started walking towards the door, he spotted it; the large white envelope lying on the end of the sofa. With little effort he slid it into the pile, under his arm, without her noticing.

Perhaps the heart attack had been provoked by the senator working too many hours? Or perhaps the white envelope which had triggered an adverse reaction in the office had produced something more serious at home? Maybe neither was related. He was going to find out.

Chapter 26

St. Augustine, Florida

Chief Fischer read through the report on his desk again. The stills of the CCTV pictures were fuzzy, not enough to decipher the car's licence plate, but clear enough to detail circumstances leading to the collision. The forensic team would do more to tidy the pictures and get the number of the car.

But even the fuzzy pictures showed the murderous intent of the driver in what was barely a timeframe of thirty seconds. In the space of a few hundred yards and for no apparent reason, the large 4X4 BMW swerved and sideswiped Irina Lukin's small Ford. The impact was stark, the attack sudden and clearly unexpected. The Ford veered violently towards the crash barrier as the driver struggled to control her small car. Surprisingly, she did manage to curb the slip before another assault. If there had been any doubt about the intentions of the BMW, it was confirmed with the second attack, more forceful than the first, resulting in the small car being rammed and crushed as it was sandwiched between its attacker and the roadside barrier. Further confirmation of the intent was the speed of the getaway.

Fischer read the timing at the bottom of each frame. It was all done in a flash; the Ford was half the width it had been before and its driver seriously injured. The policeman shook his head. A serious, dreadful crime had been committed, the evidence clear but the motive unknown.

Fischer pulled his car into the parking lot of St. Augustine hospital with a half dozen CCTV stills laid out on the passenger seat. He still didn't have a clue to the motive behind the crime but he did have some suspicions. He gathered up the stills and studied them again. He opened the mauve folder underneath the photos which contained a set of new photos.

These new pictures were much more disturbing than the ones of the crash. The first set showed a frightened girl whose face, arms and upper body took the brunt of the collision, her hair matted in blood and her face bleeding from cuts. The second batch showed her several hours later, the cuts ugly and sealed with her coagulated blood scabs and her face dotted with painful looking bruises.

Sadly, the injuries were not just cosmetic. He pulled out a sheet of paper which summarised her medical report. She had suffered internal bleeding which the surgeons dealt with immediately. The pain from her wounds, it claimed, would require potent painkillers and heavy sedation. It was nearly two days now since the crash. He was hoping to talk to her.

His cell phone rang to alert him to statements made by witnesses. He checked his tablet and downloaded the text. He shook his head in despair. Why, after the ten years he'd been in his job was he always surprised by witness statements? While some were helpful in solving crime, in his experience, they were the most inaccurate and inconsistent building blocks on which to build a case.

He read the two statements quickly. It was late afternoon when the crash had occurred and, although the light was good, neither of the statements matched. One claimed the BMW was black, the other witness wasn't sure. One swore the Ford caused the accident while the other swore the opposite. One witness was male, the other female; both in their forties. Interestingly, there was one consistent fact. They both claimed there were two men in the offending car.

It sounded like a sigh of despair and frustration as Fischer looked through the glass wall into the room where Irina Lukin was still struggling to recover.

Her attending doctor sidled up to the policeman. 'You wanted to talk to me?' he asked quietly.

Fischer nodded and steered him by an elbow away from the glass. 'When can I speak to her? She still looks in a bad way.'

'As a car crash victim, the bruising and cuts she sustained will be with her for some time but she's on the mend. When you can chat to her is up to her constitution, how well she responds.'

'Can you give me some idea? She may be my only reliable witness.'

The doctor shook his head. 'She is heavily sedated at the moment, so the effects of the drugs are likely to be evident for a few days more.'

'A few days?' repeated Fischer, louder than he intended. 'Sorry, doctor,' he added quickly with an apologetic smile. 'I was hoping......' The sentence died away but the meaning was clear enough.

The doctor returned to peer through the glass wall again. 'But she's doing fine.' He turned back to the policeman. 'I can't guarantee it, Chief, but there's every possibility that she can't remember what happened anyway.'

'Or won't,' responded Fischer immediately.

The medic shrugged and walked to the room door. 'I'll keep you informed, Chief. That's all I can promise.'

Within five minutes, Fischer was back in his car, punching the fast dial button on his cell phone. 'I'm at the hospital. I don't think we're going to get anything from the girl, at least for the moment. Did you get anything on the car?'

'No sir,' came the answer. 'I've a check out on all local garages that would tackle a repair of this kind. There are not that many, given that's what the driver decides to do. He must know it's a risk.'

'What about the registration?'

'Forensic managed the first three digits.'

Fischer thought for a moment. The pathetic sight of the injured girl flashed through his mind. It was difficult to disguise his disgust. Somehow, she'd looked so helpless, lying in the hospital bed, tied up to tubes and all the other supports. 'Run another check. Use any database you can get into. If there are any objections, let me know. The ship, what's it called, the *Orient Atlantic*, I have a feeling the answers may lie there.'

Chapter 27

St. Augustine, Florida

The researchers in the agency were a truly remarkable team; to that Darlene Shannon would certainly testify. Some were young, just sampling their first of the organisation while others were seasoned diggers whose efforts could unearth invaluable gems.

The youngsters, she found, were excited in their new environment; their energy contagious. The older ones, while experienced, were less malleable and more entrenched. There was room for both.

They would trawl through publications, academic papers, conference speeches, transcripts of broadcasts just as a matter of routine. The good ones could spot what was unusual, flag it for attention and, if categorised properly and with luck, it would find its way to the right person.

She logged into her agency's secure database. A few more codes allowed her access to the information she wanted. She wanted more than an historic record of McCabe.

His pedigree was impressive to some. To others he was an idealistic boy scout who made all sorts of waves and didn't see the bigger picture. That latter perspective was usually shared by those with blatant vested interests. It was evident that McCabe was a meddler and a nuisance who'd upset their applecarts frequently. She smiled at the quotes from some powerbrokers on Capitol Hill who couldn't disguise their loathing of the journalist who'd rocked their boat too many times. Sadly, one investigation resulted in a congressman taking his own life. The fallout was immense and even political rivals closed ranks against McCabe. He was recalled to London by his editor. Rumour had it that the journalist was outraged and the relationship with his editor never recovered.

As she read the text, she couldn't but chuckle. Sometimes, his behaviour could be considered mischievous. He was a human stalking horse, the waves he created as he lumbered his way chasing stories, invariably stirred undercurrents that disturbed many who were comfortable with the status quo. But it was his involvement in this Florida affair that concerned her.

By total fluke, he'd been a neighbour of Harry Meyer but, supposedly, they had never met. However, the dead man had held the journalist in high esteem. Her analysts claimed that he had arranged to meet McCabe in St. Augustine. But it was all rumour. Nothing was firm. She peered at the last entry.

As you know, McCabe returned to DC from St. Augustine for a short trip, apparently to search Harry Meyer's houseboat. But he had a meeting with Dwight Sanchez a low-level Agency worker who was murdered two days later, assailants unknown. We have no input regarding what he has learned.

She nodded as she read it again.

Unwittingly or not, McCabe had already begun to make waves.

Chapter 28

St. Augustine, Florida

Fischer closed the door of the lab quietly behind him.
'Are you frightened to disturb the bodies,' said Barrett, the forensic chief. He nodded to the two corpses lying on the trolleys. 'They're past caring,' he said, almost dismissively. 'I don't mean to be disrespectful but in their case, I think they've gone to a better place. Both burdened by bad luck and drugs for too long.'
Fischer walked to the far end of the lab towards the office.
'However, you're not here for them. I take it you got my report?'
Fischer sat on one of the chairs in front of the desk. 'I only read the summary. I was surprised. I wanted you to talk me through it.' The report had outlined the examination of a car found abandoned by a police patrol. It wasn't until checking its description with headquarters that they realised it was the subject of numerous alerts. 'Yes, it's the vehicle we've been looking for, alright. We're running a check on its ownership. The latest information we have claims the owner is abroad. The information is confusing.'

Fischer pulled out the photos of the car, stapled to the summary. 'I can't tell much from this. Where is it?'

'We've given it a good home.' The forensic smiled then went towards an exit which led into a large yard behind the lab.

The policeman followed.

The car was damaged much more than was apparent in the photos. The wing opposite the driver was badly crushed and scraped. Even the untrained eye could tell that it had collided with another vehicle at speed.

Fischer slowly walked round the vehicle, checking the different damage spots against the photos he held in his hand. 'The colours are not obvious in the pictures.'

'What colours?'

The policeman walked to the side of the car. 'Those,' he said pointing to the streaks on the side of the vehicle.

'You have a good eye, Chief,' said the forensic walking towards the car.

Fischer laughed. 'Thanks but any fool can see those colours,' he said pointing to the grazing.

'I wasn't talking about identifying them. It's what they mean.'

'That's obvious, is it not?'

'Sorry, Chief, I'm ahead of myself.' He walked right up to the damaged wing. 'There is evidence of collision with Irina Lukin's car, no question. But it doesn't tell the entire story.'

Fischer looked a little bemused. 'I told you I only read the summary. You'll need to elaborate.'

Barrett gave him a disapproving look. 'I'm sure I put it in.'

The policeman forced a smile. 'I'm sure you did. Talk me through it. It always helps.'

The forensic nodded, produced a small scalpel then proceeded to scrape a bit of the paintwork around the wing damage. 'Come a little closer,' he said as he wiped the scrapings onto a small white cloth. 'They're different colours,' he added without elaboration.

'That much is obvious,' said Fischer, a little sharply. The words sounded harsher than intended. He rephrased. 'What I mean is that we would have expected to find that, no?'

The forensic gave one of his characteristic chuckles again.

'Sorry, that's the scientist in me. We can be obtuse sometimes. Look closer.'

The policeman stepped forward and looked at the scraped paint on the cloth. He still looked puzzled.

'They're probably not obvious. I've had the benefit of examining them under a microscope, so I know what I'm looking for.' He spread the scrapings across the cloth. 'There are three colours here with two recent deposits.'

Fischer moved even closer and peered at the cloth. 'Are you saying what I think you are?' he asked then stopped for a moment. 'But I'm not sure what it means.'

The forensic lifted the cloth and spread it across the bonnet of the car. 'This car hit Irina Lukin's, no question. But it was also in collision with another.'

'At the same time?'

The scientist shook his head. 'It's difficult to get the precise timing. There is a small deposit of rust. I'd say not much of an interval between one and the other.'

'What interval and what do you conclude from that?'

The forensic hesitated a little, as he studied the scrapings on the cloth again. 'It would only be a guess, you understand?'

'Well?' responded Fischer, obviously impatient, pushing for an answer.

'This car hit or was in collision with another, a day or so before.'

'It had an accident before it was used as a murder weapon.'

The forensic seemed to hesitate again.

'What's the problem,' snapped Fischer.

'It's only conjecture.' He seemed a little reluctant to be pushed again for an answer.

'You've told me that already. Let's have it!'

The scientist leaned nearer the car and again pointed to the punctured metalwork. 'Judging by the extent of the damage and the violence on impact, I'd say this car has been used as a murder weapon once before.'

Fischer walked round the car again, studying the outside then peering at the interior. He opened the driver's door. 'Is it OK if I get in?'

'Sure.'

He slipped behind the wheel, looked at both wing mirrors then the rear-view. He was outside in less than a minute. 'I don't suppose you got any prints?'

'Everything was clean, except this one,' said the forensic, handing over a print. 'I think he missed it. It's on the cigarette lighter.'

'What about the owner?'

'If he's untidy you can smell the car a mile away. If he's not and cleans it regularly there are still traces around the ashtray. I'm guessing this car is not owned by a smoker. I'm also guessing the smoker who was in this car is your murderer.'

'And were there any traces around the ashtray?'

The forensic shook his head. 'No but I'll make a few more checks. We might get lucky. We'll run a few tests on the ash on the lighter filament. It always catches some traces.'

'And the fingerprint?'

'There's no ID on it yet; early days.

Chapter 29

Washington, DC

Jason Miller was at his desk early as usual. He'd already made two phone calls; one to the hospital to get an update on the welfare of his boss and a second to the senator's home.

The news from the hospital was no improvement on the night before. Apparently, the patient was still not out of danger, he had suffered a heart attack and the following twenty-four hours were critical. The severity of the attack would be measured by how quickly he responded to the hospital care which would be determined by the damage done to his heart. According to the official hospital bulletin the senator was as well as could be expected under the circumstances. He was still under heavy sedation and was unlikely to be conversing with anyone, except his doctors, for at least another day. But the prognosis was good, all the readings were positive.

The second of Miller's calls, to the senator's home in Georgetown, was less positive. The senator's wife was deeply depressed and upset. No words seemed to console her. She ranted on about a whole range of unrelated issues that suggested she felt guilty for not being at home when her husband had the attack. In the end he stopped trying and just listened to her guilt trip. She seemed to be in search of some form of absolution.

Perhaps it was therapeutic for her. He couldn't help her. In the end he fabricated an excuse and cut the conversation short.

He breathed a heavy sigh, as he ended the call. He was relieved but saddened. The woman was very distressed but he couldn't help her.

The white blank envelope lay on his desk, a haunting reminder of what had befallen his boss. But was it the cause? Was he correct in his thinking? He'd no evidence to support that theory, just a suspicion that its arrival had been accompanied by a wave of tension which swept over the senator. Had that same gloom followed him to Georgetown and provoked his heart attack?

When he'd got home the previous night, after leaving the senator's home, he'd examined the content quickly before he'd collapsed from exhaustion; the end of a tiring and emotionally draining day. His original suspicions must have been wrong, he'd thought. The content looked harmless. He couldn't think of anything less stressful than poring over a brochure of a luxury cruise ship. The opposite should surely be the case? Every picture contained smiling faces with backgrounds of more smiling faces. Surely this was heaven on earth, at least on the high seas. He hadn't changed his view this morning and was just as puzzled.

He grabbed a cup of coffee from the percolator in the corner of the office. Equipped with his first dose of caffeine that morning he was ready to tackle the envelope again. He pulled out the brochure and spread it flat on his desk. He scanned it several times. Still nothing of any consequence entered his mind. This time the brochure wouldn't easily slide back into the envelope. After three tries he pulled out the obstacle; a half column of a newspaper cutting. The story was one of many he'd prepared for the Congressman, usually those containing some item of local interest. It was from the *Washington Post*, the morning the envelope had arrived. It must have been put in by the senator himself. It was a reprint of a story filed from Florida for a British newspaper, the *London Daily Herald*.

Mystery of Dead DC Man aboard Florida Marie Celeste, screamed the headline.

The story was written by the newspaper's US Editor at Large, Mike McCabe.

Chapter 30

St. Augustine, Florida

There were no more television bulletins or online updates on the Sanchez killing. McCabe tried the Mexican's telephone number but it continued to ring without answer. If the phone was tapped, he knew he would be detected; it was a risk. Gone were the days when someone could make a telephone call and remain undiscovered. Technology made anonymity a thing of the past. Within microseconds the digits that identified him to the world could be traced and copied a million times. Then his call would be easily sourced and an electronic trail mapped right to his door. It would only be a matter of time before someone in the shadows would be mentioning his name. He'd bet they knew about him and his association with Sanchez already.

He was getting a little tired of hotel life now and missed his houseboat. He'd get back there soon. But he needed to run as much of this story to ground here, although he was at a loss where to go next. So far he'd followed leads up too many blind alleys. It was wasteful and time-consuming but there was little alternative.

His biking companion, Tracy Garrison, had been fun and helpful. After Flagler she'd decided to return to Daytona Beach, her project done. Now she wanted to restart her life with her loser boyfriend. She'd shown no interest in pursuing the story any further.

The meeting with the Flagler professor had been interesting and they'd established that *The Georgia* had followed a similar route to the *Orient Atlantic*. Given the marine traffic that sailed in those waters there was probably a host of sailing craft that crossed the major shipping and cruising lanes frequently. But what did it mean? He was much more concerned with the death of Sanchez. He'd put a call into DC and was waiting for some response. That source might provide a lead.

He looked at his watch. It was mid-afternoon and he hadn't had a drink. That was easily rectified. A few ice cubes clinked at the bottom of the glass and came to a halt as he splashed a generous Black Label measure on top.

His cell phone buzzed before he could sample it. The number didn't look familiar. Caller ID was next to useless in his profession. Ignoring unidentified calls was not a habit to be cultivated. His number was in a host of listings. Anyone could get the number from his London or DC office. That's the way he operated. The one he didn't answer might be the one he regretted.

He pressed the receive button but the call went dead; a caller having second thoughts or just a wrong connection? He'd never know. Ten minutes later he got the call he'd been expecting. It was brief and the content not surprising. There would be no police announcement or presence in the Sanchez case. It was being handled by the FBI and cloaked in some security blanket.

That was the official line. He didn't like it. He didn't like anything behind closed doors and certainly he railed against anything that smelled of clandestine government. His source rang off without any apology.

Chapter 31

Washington, DC

Jason Miller was unsure what to do now. He knew there was something wrong. Maybe he had misread the situation? Perhaps it wasn't the discovery of the envelope on his desk that had caused the senator's concern and when he took it home his heart attack was just a spooky coincidence? But he didn't think so. The senator was no fool and while he hadn't confided in him, he knew there was some connection.

He had heard the name of the cruise ship before. He remembered a phone call, several weeks ago, which had come from the main switchboard while the senator was out of the office.

The caller sounded distressed but said she'd call back. An hour later when the senator had returned, she did.

The senator seemed surprised to get the call and had closed the door to the inner office before he continued to speak to her. Miller heard nothing.

The same girl rang two days later, again when the senator was out. As previously, she didn't leave a message and said she'd call back. This time, she never did.

Miller was trying to put together snippets of things he may have missed, previous occasions when he'd seen the senator agitated. The cutting he'd found in the white envelope about the death of Harry Meyer was a reminder.

The television channels had given the story little coverage. The senator had trawled the networks looking for more news on the death and had asked Miller to do the same. Why? He didn't know. The congressman gave him no more information.

He now read the newspaper cutting from the envelope several times. It didn't say any more than had been reported in the frugal broadcasts. The name of the writer, Mike McCabe, had been highlighted in ink, presumably by the senator. Did that mean anything?

He waited until lunchtime when the office was relatively quiet. He would have a chance to check a few things without being disturbed or his computer screen being overlooked.

When all was clear, he typed in a few instructions. The search wasn't difficult. Mike McCabe's profile was lengthy. It was impressive to some. To others his actions were irresponsible, interfering and provocative. He was deemed by a few on Capitol Hill to be in breach of his privileges as a visiting journalist. He also guessed the senator would have been among the minority supporting the journalist's stance.

Getting McCabe's cell phone number was surprisingly easy. The main DC number of his newspaper was listed next to his website biography. One call and he'd got the journalist's direct line. He had dialled the number but at the sound of a voice at the other end, he froze. Whether courage failed him or his resolve was undermined, he didn't know. But he had pressed the red button.

The call had been an impulsive act. It wasn't clear in his mind what he expected to get from it. He supposed he might talk to the journalist, get some more information about the background to Meyer's death in the hope that it could give him a clue to his boss's involvement. But the logic was unconvincing.

He sat staring at his cell phone. The senator, he knew, was not a man who would easily panic. Nor was he a collector of cuttings. The newspaper article on Meyer had some significance. He was convinced it was tied to the brochure and possibly the girl caller. But he was at a loss to come up with any feasible explanation. He ran his hand across the brochure to flatten it on the desk. Did he expect that the touch might inspire him, give him some spiritual insight into its meaning or the motive of the sender? Now, that idea was even more fanciful.

His index finger rested on the telephone number of the local travel agent at the bottom of the brochure. He thought for a moment then dialled the number. It was answered immediately, catching him unawares. He didn't have his thoughts in order and was ready to hang up. 'Can I help you?' was the polite response.

He stuttered some words. 'I...I....my...my boss got a brochure through the post the other day,' he said quickly.

'Which one?'

'It was about a cruise ship called the *Orient Atlantic*.'

There was silence at the end of the phone for a moment. 'You know, that's very strange. We've had several enquiries about that ship in the last few days. One was very sad; a client of ours, who'd been on the ship, died recently.'

'Oh, I'm sorry,' he said instinctively, without knowing his next move.

'It was in all the newspapers. I even got a call from the police in Florida.' The agent lowered his voice, almost to a whisper, as if he was sharing a confidence. 'Yes. He was found dead on a yacht in Florida,' seemingly uninhibited about sharing the tit-bit. Miller lifted the cutting from his desk. 'His name wouldn't be Harry Meyer, would it?'

He agent's voice returned to normal. 'I couldn't say, sir. Client confidentiality, you know.'

He paused for a moment. 'Of course, you didn't get that from me.'

Miller had found the connection he'd been seeking. The travel agent had told him nothing but had told him everything. It didn't need to be spelled out. The message was clear. That was more than enough, at least for the moment. 'Thanks,' he said quietly then pressed the button to finish the call.

Chapter 32

St. Augustine, Florida

There is no doubt about it, said the scrawled note on Chief Fischer's desk. Check the coverage yourself. You'll find it in the database video file; access in the usual way.

Fischer brought his computer to life. There were two collisions, considered to be similar to each other, selected for his inspection. The second was the Lukin assault where the 4X4 was easily identified.

He focused on the first. The lighting was dim so the pictures were poor. However, the action was clear enough. In the footage, the victim's car bounced off the roadside safety barrier. It was a dark green Toyota and the driver braked hard but appeared unable to avoid further damage. It continued to scrape its way along the barrier; its registration plate quite clear.

Fischer leaned back in his chair and read the additional information on the bottom of the memo. *Address below, his name is Charlie Shepherd.*

The telephone rang. 'Chief, I've just finished checking on the collisions. Have you looked at the videos?'

'I have.'

'No doubt it's the same 4X4 BMW which sideswiped Irina Lukin but no ID on its driver. There's still some confusion over the car's ownership.'

'Why?'

Fischer could hear the rustle of a notebook. 'It was part of a rental stock in Miami until about a month ago then sold at auction. It was bought for cash but wasn't reregistered before it was stolen while the owner went on holiday.'

'Well that doesn't tell us much, does it?'

'There is one more thing; more information on the man we suspect was the first victim. The driver's name is *Charlie Shepherd*. There is no indication why he left but until about a month ago, he worked as a steward on the *Orient Atlantic*.

Fischer brought the car to a stop at the top of a narrow lane, flanked by overgrown bushes which scraped his bonnet as he parked. He could see the buildings about two hundred yards to his right, an old construction to which an extension had been added recently. He guessed by its appearance that it was once a school or something similar. It had that cloistered look.

He checked the map spread out on the passenger seat and matched it with his GPS readings. This was supposedly the home of *Charlie Shepherd*. He pushed the car door open, walked to the rusty wrought-iron gate, leaned hard against its stubbornness to open then walked up the gravel path.

The old part of the house and the extension had been converted into luxury apartments with a 24-hour manned security desk.

'No visitor is allowed access without an appointment,' said the deskman pretentiously.

The uniformed Police Chief ignored the comment. 'You can show me or I'll find it myself,' he said without the slightest emotion in his voice.

The security man lifted the telephone by his side and punched a few digits.

Fischer stepped forward, bent over the desk and brought a heavy right hand down onto the telephone base. 'You really don't want to be doing that,' he said staring at the man. 'I'll be happy to give him a surprise,' he added and feigned a smile.

The deskman returned the phone to rest. 'I'll take you along.'

An elevator ride to the next level, a short walk and they stood outside the apartment. Two rings on the doorbell were followed by too long a wait. Another two rings, a little more prolonged than the others, still produced no response.

The noise of the elevator coming to rest at the end of the corridor breached the quiet.

Fischer saw a man emerge. He walked up to them without saying a word then opened the door. 'Can I help you,' he said, almost casually.

'Mr. Shepherd,' greeted the manager. 'I'm sorry....'

The policeman interrupted. 'If you have a moment, Mr. Shepherd,' Fischer said softly, while looking down the hallway. 'Inside would be better.'

Shepherd said nothing but walked into the apartment, leaving the door open.

'Thank you. I'll take it from here.' Fischer nodded to the manager, walked through the door and closed it. The hallway inside was dimly lit but he could see Shepherd in front walking towards what was probably the lounge.

'Not another parking ticket,' Shepherd joked. The laughter sounded a little nervous. 'I'm going to have a drink, would you like anything?' he said walking towards a small cabinet beside the window then pouring a drink.

The policeman shook his head. 'I am not here about a traffic offence.'

Shepherd looked puzzled. He laughed. 'I was joking,' he added.

Fischer hesitated for a moment. He was trying to select his words carefully. 'A car was sideswiped two days ago, on the freeway, and the driver seriously injured. One of the cars belonged to you.' Strictly speaking it was the truth, although they were two separate incidents. He was testing the water and feeling his way towards some reaction, he hoped.

Shepherd wasn't smiling anymore. 'I don't understand. There must be some mistake.'

The policeman pulled out his notebook. 'You do drive a dark green Toyota?' He read the registration to him without waiting for an answer. Fischer ensured it sounded very formal.

Shepherd dropped quietly onto the sofa. He looked confused and was trying to interpret what had been said. 'Yes, I drive a dark green Toyota,' he repeated, apparently still trying to decipher the meaning behind the policeman's words. He seemed stunned, looking for an explanation.

Fischer had got the reaction he wanted. Clearly, Shepherd was disorientated. 'You didn't report it,' he added quickly. 'When someone is injured, it is an offence to leave the scene of an accident.' He was laying it on with a trowel.

Shepherd seemed to get a second wind, rose to his feet, went to the cabinet again and poured himself another drink. 'I think you're confusing things. I was sideswiped and barely managed to control my car. But I wasn't injured and the other driver took off.'

Fischer felt the fish had just got off the hook. Not for long, he said to himself. 'Why didn't you report it?'

Shepherd took a large gulp from his new drink. 'There was no damage and I wasn't injured.'

Fischer studied him for a moment.

Shepherd was back on the sofa. The drinks from the cabinet had given his nerves a boost, but he was still on edge.

Fischer wasn't going to play games anymore. 'It didn't bother you that someone had tried to kill you?' The policeman's words were blunt. He was hoping the effects would be the same.

'That seems strange to me. Why would anyone do that? Most people would be phoning the police in seconds, unless they had something to hide.'

Shepherd gave another nervous laugh. His drink hadn't been effective enough. It wasn't able to muffle the fear in his voice. Fischer's trained ears could detect that sound through lead. He'd heard enough of it over the years. He said nothing more but stared straight ahead at Shepherd. He could feel the atmosphere getting tenser. That was the strategy.

'Tried to kill me?' Shepherd asked. His voice had gone up an octave. 'That's ludicrous. What makes you think that?'

The policeman knew his timing was right. But the punchlines had to be delivered with the same finesse. 'Because the same vehicle tried to kill Irina Lukin.'

Shepherd's mouth dropped open. He looked as if he'd been hit by something very heavy and unexpected. He stared blankly at the policeman.

Fischer moved in for the kill. 'She's in hospital fighting for her life.'

Shepherd dropped his now empty glass onto the carpet and cupped his head in his hands.

The policeman stepped forward and touched him on the shoulder which was visibly shaking.

Shepherd's face remained covered for several moments but then he seemed to recover. 'Where is she?' he asked quickly, drying what looked like moisture below his eyes.

Fischer said nothing. He didn't know how valuable a bargaining tool he had, if at all. It was cruel what he needed to do. But it had to be done. There were no easy decisions in this game. 'I can't disclose that. She is under police protection,' he said while lifting the empty glass from the floor. 'Given the severity of her injuries, we have no choice.' He delivered the lines in as sombre a tone as he could manage.

Shepherd appeared to have another thought. 'Do you think they'll try again?' He sounded even more frightened now.

Fischer watched him carefully. He had his man where he wanted him but he had to reel him in carefully or the chance would be gone. He paused as he watched the frightened figure in front of him, still visibly shaking. But he needed to go for the jugular. He had no choice. He said nothing for a moment and let the tension build. He had to try his luck and push for an answer. 'They'll probably try again, don't you think? You do know who they are?'

Shepherd recoiled for a moment. He seemed surprised if not startled by the questions. His expression said it all. He shook his head from side to side, as if debating with his inner self. The outburst was unexpected. 'I didn't think they would go that far.' 'Who?' pressed Fischer. 'Who do you think is responsible? They tried to kill her and nearly succeeded'. He was piling on the theatrical as much as he could. 'They tried to kill you.'

Shepherd was blitzed now.

Fischer went for broke. He didn't know the connection but he was going to take a chance. The guilt card was always worth playing. 'Surely you must have known she would be next.'

Shepherd was obviously struggling to find the words. 'I didn't think they'd go that far; I didn't think they'd go that far......' he kept repeating. He was rambling, murmuring the same phrase over and over.

There were some other words which Fischer didn't catch. He moved closer. Had he now a lever to extract the information Shepherd was so carefully guarding?

Shepherd started again. 'I didn't think.........' He stopped suddenly then looked up. 'I need to go to her,' he insisted. Clearly, Shepherd was now totally distraught.

Chapter 33

St. Augustine, Florida

Chief Fischer watched the entrance to the hospital complex, just outside St. Augustine, from his unmarked police car. It had been many years since he'd been on surveillance duty. What he expected to get from this reconnaissance was anybody's bet. Nevertheless, it was one he was banking on.

He'd planted the seed in Charlie Shepherd's mind, one he hoped would flower. It was apparent from his reaction to the news of Irina's condition that he was upset, that they'd been close and it had shocked him. Whether the emotional reaction would be enough for him to disclose to the police what he knew was a different question.

But Fischer didn't need to be an ace detective to know that Shepherd was scared and that something was forcing his silence. He doubted whether it was any power the police had which was causing his fear.

Undoubtedly it was the information Shepherd guarded, secrets or confidences he shared with others, that he now believed put him in danger. But his fear for the safety of Irina appeared to be a prominent factor. They were close, no doubt.

Fischer was gambling that the steward's anxiety for his own safety would be overridden by his concern for the girl. The policeman sat upright in the car. His gamble had paid off. The game had just begun.

Charlie Shepherd pulled his car up about a hundred yards away at the other side of the parking lot, got out, inspected the building, locked the car and made his way to the entrance. Undoubtedly, he was on his way to see Irina.

Fischer was on his cell phone within seconds. Two men were outside the elevator on the victim's floor. There were two more on the seats that flanked Irina's room, all in plain clothes. The Police Chief was giving Shepherd easy access to the crash victim.

He had hoped Shepherd would come to see her at the hospital, so far so good. He'd also wagered that the sight of the poor girl, her bruising, her cuts and the medical lashings which supported her would loosen his tongue. He doubted the steward would present any danger to the girl. As a precaution, he'd ordered the door to her room to be locked.

It would take about five minutes for Shepherd to get to the fifth floor and probably another minute or two to get to the room. His every move would be watched by the guarding policeman. That was the plan.

Fischer looked at his watch impatiently. He knew it was a gamble which could backfire. Instead of the sight of the injured girl guaranteeing disclosure, it could have the opposite effect. Shepherd could clam up, become even more frightened and hightail it to the nearest exit. The policeman looked at his watch again. By now, Shepherd should be getting out of the elevator.

There would be no phone call from the police-guards to Fischer until Shepherd had seen the girl. It was his reaction to the girl's condition which was the key. Those were the policeman's orders; that was the plan.

If it worked, the final part of the strategy would unfold naturally. Fischer would meet a distraught Shepherd as he left the hospital and question him again; this time with more success. It sounded simple but he knew there were a few improbabilities and they rested on the steward's reaction. It was a calculated risk. The odds were on his side, at least in theory.

Fischer looked at his watch yet again. Perhaps Shepherd was just staring through the glass at the victim and paralysed at the sight? Maybe the anticipated response would not come? There was every possibility that the steward was so frightened he'd run for cover anyway?

Fischer was getting worried. He pressed a button on his cell phone. His voice was raised and his tone curt. 'What do you mean he hasn't arrived?' He looked at his watch yet again. 'He left here fifteen minutes ago. It couldn't have taken him that long. Close the floor down, no one in or out until I say otherwise then find him.' There was something seriously wrong. He could sense it.

He pushed the car door open and ran to the entrance. There were dozens of people amassed in the hallway beside the main elevator. Some were staring at the ground others were shouting; many screaming. It was chaos. He pushed his way through to the elevator. Lying across the open sliding doors was a bloodied body. He didn't need a forensic eye to know the person had been shot and was dead. Despite the mess, the body was easily identifiable. It was Charlie Shepherd.

About twenty feet to the left of the elevator with a clear view of the body was Darlene Shannon. She'd just returned her gun to its holster. Unlike the others surrounding the body, she didn't look in the least bit surprised.

She walked slowly past the crowd pushing each other, rubbernecking to see if they could get a better view and a frenzied-looking Police-Chief trying to make sense of the chaos.

Five minutes later she started her car up and pressed one of the buttons on her cell phone's pre-programmed directory. 'He's dead, no debate, shot at the hospital. We now have another problem.' She stopped for a moment to ponder. 'The girl; she's all that's left.'

For McCabe the story had turned rancid with Irina Lukin still fighting for her life.

Police Chief Fischer was on the phone to him again. Did he know Charlie Shepherd, a steward and supposedly one of her closest friends on the cruise ship? 'He was brutally murdered in the hospital entrance, on his way to see Lukin,' he reported. 'He was shot, no witnesses. The place is as busy as Times Square and nobody saw anything; unbelievable!'

McCabe felt frustrated too. His original motivation was to find out who killed Harry Meyer, the neighbour with whom he'd barely had a conversation; most of those exchanges reserved for transient greeting or a hand-wave. Now the story had become much more complex. What did these young people know about someone who'd turned up dead, floating on a stolen yacht with McCabe's hotel details scrawled on a newspaper cutting?

What Meyer was doing afloat the craft was an obvious first question but there were dozens of other supplementary ones now. Why had Meyer's houseboat been burgled; who did it, and what were they after? The break-in could have been coincidental; this was a big city after all. The crime was far from uncommon. McCabe's news antennae didn't believe it. It was like an itch he couldn't scratch, a thirst he couldn't satisfy.

'I don't know if the DC police are interested but I'm going to send our findings through to them. Given Meyer came from there, that's got to be worthwhile,' concluded Fischer.

The phone call that went dead was another thing nagging McCabe. Like everyone in God's creation, he'd received spurious telephone calls; some misdirected, some the handiwork of an automated marketing robot. But somehow he felt there was a real person at the end of the call. He had nothing to support that conclusion, nothing logical, just a sense that there was a real person at the other end of the telephone who'd taken cold feet.

He dialled the news desk. 'Hi, it's McCabe.'

'I know,' said the surly secretary at the other end. 'Can I help?' she asked in an equally emotionless manner.

She should really do something about her telephone manner, thought McCabe. He wouldn't tell her that; she would get even more prickly. But she was damned efficient, a remarkable researcher and reliable. He forced himself to smile before he asked her. 'Did you give my telephone number to anyone in the last day or two?' He gritted his teeth. The question sounded challenging. It wasn't meant to be.

She said nothing for a moment. 'If the name didn't come up on your caller ID, there was a good chance the number came from me, don't you think?' She was on form today, that unrecognisable alternative to diplomacy.

McCabe hesitated. He wasn't sure if the question was meant to be rhetorical. 'I'll take your guidance on this,' he said diplomatically.

'I'll check my log,' she responded quickly.

'Log?' he queried quickly.

She sighed. 'You really have to try and join this century McCabe.'

He couldn't prevent himself from laughing. He thought he was doing well with his tablet and cell phone. Clearly not!

She was well ahead of his game. 'I used to have to keep a book with the callers' names and telephone numbers. In those days I had to take their word for who they were. Now, there's no need.'

'You'll have to elaborate on that,' he commented sounding slightly puzzled.

She sighed again in frustration. 'Now, the number comes up on my screen, time and name. It logs automatically.'

'Did you get a name?'

'He was a bit reluctant but after I told him it wouldn't take me a minute to find out his ID anyway, he seemed resigned to it.'

'To what?'

'Giving his name; are you listening McCabe?'

'I thought you said......'

She interrupted. 'I think I'm going to send you on a basic IT course,' she said, quite clearly enjoying her joke.

McCabe said nothing. The banter had gone far enough.

'Our system here tells me the telephone number but no more. I had to bluff the rest.'

He could well imagine her fake performance; she'd be convincing.

'The call was from the office of Senator Viktor Segal, Democrat from Virginia. The caller was one of his secretaries, a Jason Miller.'

'Did he say what he wanted?'

'I was told not to put callers under any pressure. I asked if it was in relation to a story. He said yes. Well he would say that anyway. It's a pointless instruction.' She was getting surly again. 'I ran a name check on his boss. That was the guy who had a heart attack in his home in Georgetown a few days ago.'

The Washington connection had just resurfaced. He had a feeling that was where this story would unfold. Also, he'd had his fill of hotel living in Florida.

There was also someone in DC, who might, just might, be able to correct his bearings. He brought up the directory on his cell phone, scanned the listing and picked out her name. He hadn't seen Sharon Grant for quite some time. If for no other reason, it would be fun.

Chapter 34

Washington, DC

Jason Miller had debated the issues a dozen times and he hadn't come to any real conclusion or planned a strategy. However he did know that he had to do something. He needed help, so did his boss who was still in Georgetown Hospital on the critical list. Given the senator's age, now in his late sixties, added to the stress and the demands of his lifestyle, it was probably no surprise there would be some medical price to pay. The arrival of the envelope, its contents but above all the congressman's reaction to it would suggest something different. None of those incidents may have had any connection. Even if the attack hadn't been triggered by any of these events, there was something worrying his boss. He intended to find out what.

By five o'clock the office would be empty. The other staff would have gone and most of the personnel in the adjacent offices would have drifted home. He waited. By five thirty he was confident he wouldn't be interrupted. He locked the outer door. His intention was to search the senator's inner office. The majority of the office files were contained in two locked cabinets, the contents of which contained nothing of importance, which was why the senator allowed him duplicate keys. Most of the content had been filed by him. But there were two other smaller units where the senator's personal papers were kept.

These were secured by a combination lock. More by luck than planning he'd stumbled across the code several months before. Although he'd had reservations about using the knowledge, he had no reservations now. The congressman had other files in his home in Georgetown to which he had no access, but he'd bet most were duplicates of his personal files.

He closed the door carefully behind him in the inner office. The locks on the cabinets responded to the codes and popped open without difficulty. He didn't know what he was expecting to find. This was a fishing trip. He was sure of one thing. There was not going to be a note outlining the reason why the senator had been upset and another that explained why he'd had a heart attack. At best he might find fragments.

Most of the content was predictable and were copies of the general files with the senator's comments in the margins plus a few draft speeches; nothing that would give a clue to the reason behind the senator's disturbance. Then he found what he was looking for; a small file with handwritten notes at the back of the cabinet. He wouldn't have time to study it now.

He leaned across the desk to switch the lamp off, but something caught his eye as he walked towards the door. It was a small bookmark inside the senator's diary. He pulled it out gently. It was a narrow strip of blue coloured cardboard with a ribbon on the end. In the senator's recognisable handwriting was the name Harry Meyer. That was the second reference to this dead man. The cutting in the envelope with the travel brochure was no accident then? The newspaper clipping wasn't something that had been put aside casually. It demonstrated a definite interest and intent. The man had some significance, was clearly important to the senator, as was his untimely death. He switched off the lamp, closed the inner door then locked the outer one. The search had not been in vain.

Chapter 35

Washington, DC

The *Old Ebbitt Grill* was busy as usual, with a long line waiting outside for tables and the bar two deep in bodies, waving for attention, trying to shout their orders over the din. McCabe, just in from Florida, needed a drink. He'd arrived before the busy wave; a perfect storm of tourists. The local offices added to the bedlam, decanting their labour after a week at the political front. It was a block from the White House, and just a few from the governmental administrative bureaucrats who ran the city and, by definition, the country.

McCabe had already ordered a tray of oysters, the speciality of the house. The bar was one of his favourite haunts, so it was difficult to refuse any invitation to hang out there. Unfortunately it was the same for most of the punters who squeezed their way into the place most nights of the week.

Since 1756, when it was a modest boarding house, its history claims it to have been used by Presidents until now. He took the PR with a large pinch of salt. As they say in his business: *If it's not true it should be.* There was no surprise then that tourist flocked in their thousands to the place. Politicos with intent and ambition to expand their social and contacts network by being seen in the right place also were counted among the regulars. McCabe laughed at the thought. Perhaps he was one too.

He got a glimpse of her as she came through the door, her tall figure and striking features would be noticed in any company. Sharon Grant was a cop. Not just any cop but one whose responsibilities were to provide protection for Congressmen. She'd been a regular police officer, patrolling the beat in some of the more dangerous backwaters of the Capitol and had been in a skirmish or two, where she came out on top. She was fairly accomplished in traditional martial arts but had no inhibitions about kicking an opponent in the nuts. She'd demonstrated that subtle art form on more than one occasion when an adversary found his life changed forever and his sex life halted for several months. It was no surprise then that she was headhunted to join the US Capitol Police with responsibility to protect the powerbrokers on the Hill.

She dropped down onto the stool he'd kept for her beside him at the bar.

'I needed your skills to keep this seat free from this marauding pack,' McCabe said as she sat down.

She smiled politely at the man beside her who looked ready to pounce. She didn't look in the least bit ruffled as she turned her back on him.

McCabe chuckled to himself again. 'Good to see you,' he said as he pecked her on both cheeks. 'Americans are getting very European in their behaviour,' he said, still chuckling.

'The cheek-kissing habit, you mean? I suspect that'll be banned soon too.'

'I got a tray of their best oysters,' he said, nodding at the tray. 'But the backroom is clear, so it might be a good idea if we move in there. At least we can chat.'

'I didn't realize romance was your style, Mike,' she responded, not quite able to disguise a smirk. She slid elegantly off the stool and followed him.

He ignored the remark.

A minute later they'd worked their way out of the main bar area and saw their places filled immediately like some human quicksand. A waiter followed them with the oysters.

'I see you're still on the scotch, Black Label I suppose, part of your balanced diet?'

He swirled the ice round in his glass. 'What else? I assume you'll have vodka with ice and a little hint of lemon, as usual?'

'What else?

He gave the waiter her order. 'I'll have another,' he added quickly.

'So why did you get me here? I assume it wasn't to smooch in a cubbyhole at the Ebbitt?'

'Segal,' he answered quickly. He hesitated a little, not quite sure how much he should tell her. There was no question of distrust. He just didn't want to compromise her. But hell, he'd known her long enough.

It was more than five years since he'd first met her. It was at a conference. She had been explaining to the assembled congressmen what her job was and how it could be made more effective. Most who had attended were obviously cynical and considered the lecture a waste of their valuable time. But even the diehards were convinced after her talk. She illustrated her points with close shaves in the USA and Europe and how a little more thought could prevent a tragedy.

She didn't respond to his prompt. She was listening but her eyes were on the waiter, scurrying towards her with her drink.

'You must have had some effect on that young man, that's the quickest delivery I've seen here,' he said as the waiter got to the table and placed the vodka in front of her. He'd been smitten.

'Segal,' repeated McCabe. 'Something tells me there's more to this story.'

She sampled her drink. 'And the waiter got it right. I trust you'll give him a healthy tip?'

'Segal,' he said again.

'What's your interest, Mike? Tell me when can we have a level playing field?'

'I wasn't sure how much to tell you, in case any of it compromised you. I think he's part of a story I'm working on.'

She sipped her drink for a moment. 'When are you not on a story?'

He nodded slightly with a laugh. 'I'll give you that.'

'You'll have to give me a lot more, if you want anything from me.' She was brutally frank.

He nodded again. This time there was no laughter. He told her about Meyer turning up dead on the stolen yacht in Florida.

'I know that Mike. I saw the story; you wrote it, remember?'

He looked a little embarrassed. Of course she knew that and a lot more. That was why he was here. But he didn't have the real story; another reason why he was here.

'Mike, I know the game you play and the constraints. Level with me.'

He was always reluctant to give too much away. If he'd discovered it, he'd protected it, as he did his sources. It was sometimes difficult to separate them. If he wasn't careful, one could lead to another.

'Don't neighbours like to meet up with each other on vacation? Is that so extraordinary?' She was being mischievous, if not obtuse.

He knew she'd play games, if he let her. He ignored her comment. 'He had no ID, just a newspaper cutting with my hotel details scrawled on it,' he said bluntly. There was an edge to his voice. For a moment he sounded a little testy.

She took another sip of her vodka, studying his face carefully. She was debating something within herself. 'I know all that too,' she added. 'Tell me something I don't.'

He smiled then laughed. Of course, she would have access to police files, DC and Florida, if she wanted. But she wouldn't have done it had she not been interested. That told him something. 'Why were you interested? That's an even better question.'

She liked McCabe. Too much, she suspected. It wasn't easy to forget his homing news antennae and his automatic reflexes for a story. She also had a job to do. 'You still haven't told me what you want from me Mike. What's your interest in Segal? You'll have to put it on the table.'

He hesitated again about the story. It was so incomplete. 'Meyer was an ex-navy man with a fine record and an even finer future. But he leaves the service, for no apparent reason. I think he was undercover when he was murdered. I have no idea what he was doing or why. Do you? Somewhere in this, Segal has an interest. Do you know what that was?''

She kept sipping her drink, more to give her time to think, he suspected. He could only push her so far. The very nature of her job prevented her opening up too much. She'd tell him only what she wanted and in her own time. She wouldn't tell him everything she knew. She was never a source for him but someone who was knowledgeable and gave him background or insight. In journalism both individuals could be valuable.

'So what's the Segal connection?' she asked, avoiding his question. She was testing how much he knew, if anything.

He nodded, as if he'd expected her reaction. She was answering a question with a question. But he didn't have too much information anyway. What he had was half-baked. Was it worthwhile trying to test a theory with her? If he had one, it might be an option. What did his information amount to anyway; a murdered man who'd drifted into a Florida harbour aboard a stolen yacht, and an insignificant piece of newspaper in his possession with hotel details scrawled on it? What about Meyer's boat in DC? It was evident it had been ransacked. Was that just a common break-in or something else? Then there was the senator. Someone in his office had made an attempt to contact him then lost his nerve. Was that a coincidence too? 'I don't know, that's why I'm here,' he conceded, a little reluctantly.

'So you want all the answers from me?'

'Do you know any?' he asked quickly.

She sipped her vodka then went into silent mode again.

'I got a call, or at least our news-desk did, from one of Segal's secretaries, shortly after he had a heart attack. When pushed, the caller claimed he was phoning about the dead man, or at least about the story I wrote about him. His boss had just suffered a heart attack. There may be no correlation between these events but my instincts tell me different.'

'That's why you're here?'

'This is your patch. If anything happens in it, you know about it.'

She smiled, as if acknowledging the compliment. 'Jason Miller,' she said quickly. 'We knew about him calling you too.'

Suddenly, he felt like a fish on a hook; more accurately, the bait. He looked a little annoyed.

'Sorry Mike. I had to push you. To find out what you knew.' It sounded like a genuine apology. She finished her drink and stood up to go. 'Segal was in intelligence before he came to the Senate. It's very much the invisible print in his biog.' She hesitated for a moment as if to check what she'd said. 'Knowing you, Mike, you've already stirred the pot by just being you, the dogged newshound. I can't tell you much more but be careful. I have my suspicions.'

He reacted quickly. He knew she took risks but to get her to open up on some issues was next to impossible. He sensed she wanted to say more but was constrained by her own perception of duty. He admired her for that but it made her a lousy source.

She sensed he wanted more. 'It's above my pay scale, Mike. Sorry! Protection is my bag. The security agencies deal with the other issues.'

'What other issues?'

She looked at him sternly.

He knew what the security agencies did. He didn't need it spelled out. He'd got the picture.

She smiled, as if relieved that she didn't have to elucidate. 'It wasn't a heart attack. Segal was seriously assaulted. But we don't know who nor why. Those details have been kept quiet.'

'What about his wife, she would have noticed, surely?'

'She was in such a panic. If she suspected, she's never said.'

'And Miller, what would he want with me?'

She smiled as she turned. 'Don't leave it so long next time.'

He watched her edge her way through the throng to the exit. As expected, a few heads turned to give their admiring glances, as she slipped through the bodies by the bar.

She had been guarded. In itself, that told him something and between the verbal jousting she'd dropped a few useful hints. A few more fragments had just fallen into place but the picture was still far from clear.

Chapter 36

Washington, DC

The security guard judiciously checked the monitor screening the baggage as it flowed through the sensors. McCabe walked through the arch and triggered the alarm. Frustrated he stepped back, pulled out a set of keys from his pocket, apologised to the deadpan security guard then tried again.

Visiting any government building these days was a chore. The Senate building hadn't yet got to the level adopted by the airports, although the armed security guards always looked menacing. There was nothing relaxing about visiting your local congressman.

McCabe showed his Press Card. He was ready with a reason to explain his visit. For some reason, he was never asked. His baggage trundled its way through the scanning machine and emerged at the other side, a little bashed but otherwise unharmed. Not so himself; he always felt his personal space violated. He knew it was necessary but gone were the days when your ID was good enough and you could pass a pleasant ten minutes chatting to the guards.

McCabe picked up his bag and made his way through the catacombs of the US seat of government. Although he'd been there dozens of times, the marble and veneer surroundings, while impressive, seemed out of keeping with the intentions of the Founding Fathers. He guessed he was just being pedantic. The large door to the entrance of Senator Segal's office was equally impressive. Whether the oversized doors were meant to intimidate, he wasn't sure, but they certainly made the visitor look small.

He looked at his watch. If his calculations were right, the office staff would be packing up for the night. He was taking a chance. The outer door was slightly open and the two desks immediately ahead were empty. At the far end, a girl was putting on her coat and making for the door. She smiled at him as she passed without saying a word. As she got to the door she smiled. 'He's in there,' she said nodding towards the door of the inner office.

'Come in Mr.McCabe,' said a voice from the inner office. McCabe was surprised. He walked through the doorway.

A young man was just closing a filing cabinet. The drawer banged as he slammed it shut then walked towards McCabe.

'Jason Miller,' he said with his right hand extended in greeting. 'I expected you to turn up, sooner or later. I did alert our security people at the front. They rang me when you came through,' he said pointing to one of two chairs that flanked the desk. 'Do sit down. I knew it wouldn't take you long to find me.'

'It wasn't much of a challenge with technology; nothing seems invisible these days.'

'I suppose not; makes your job that much easier, I suppose?' Miller said, almost light-heartedly. 'How can I help you?'

McCabe was taken by surprise. Surely that was his question? 'I'm sorry,' he said slowly. 'I thought you wanted to talk to me?' 'Yes but nothing we couldn't have done on the phone. I just wanted more information on the dead man you wrote about.' He gave the impression he was struggling to recall his name. 'Ah, yes,' he said, as if he'd just remembered. 'Harry Meyer; now it has come back to me.'

McCabe was immediately uneasy. This conversation didn't make any sense. Miller had either changed his mind or, more likely, it had been changed for him.

Clearly, Miller read the surprised expression on McCabe's face. 'The senator is always interested in incidents that might raise security issues,' he said in an attempt to dismiss any suggestion that his enquiry was unusual.

'What would they be?' responded McCabe immediately.

'Potential, I mean, potential security issues,' countered Miller quickly. 'That's why I wanted more information. But I gather that's not the case.'

'From whom?' responded McCabe, instinctively, like a spring uncoiling.

Miller said nothing. He just smiled benignly. 'Sorry to have caused you any trouble. You see, the senator likes to have all the information on tap. That's my job,' he said, satisfied with the explanation.

McCabe smiled to himself. This performance was a sham. It told him someone was trying to stop this ball rolling. But he'd been there before when a source, for whatever reason, got cold feet, had second-thoughts or more likely had been got at, either threatened or cajoled in some way or other. He'd have to work a little harder, that's all. He stood up, as if to leave. The gesture was meant to relieve any pressure on the young man. 'Oh, I am sorry to have intruded,' he said apologetically.

Miller looked immediately relieved.

McCabe had no intention of leaving until he had at least some inkling into what provoked the young man's telephone call. He'd also like to know why he was backing off. He didn't have much to go on but Miller didn't know that. 'The senator was in hospital with a heart attack when you attempted to contact me. That timing was a little out, was it not? I doubt if the congressman would then have been interested in any press cuttings. You were after something else. What was that?'

Miller looked a little confused. 'I still run his office,' he said quickly. 'He'll be returning to fitness soon,' he added, not sounding in the least bit convincing and struggling to find any credible rationale. He looked uncomfortable.

Whether he could bluff it out, McCabe wasn't sure. But he had to take a gamble that Miller hadn't been fully briefed on the senator's condition or about the circumstances in which he had suffered his injuries.

'The senator was seriously assaulted, if not an attempt was made on his life,' McCabe said quickly. 'It wasn't a heart attack. I assume you're aware of that?' The disclosure was a gamble but it would test how much Miller knew, if anything and his reaction to the news. McCabe was betting that he hadn't been told. He was hoping. The effect would then be more prominent.

Miller looked surprised. He stared blankly ahead.

McCabe pushed further. This could be a good source but he needed to be persuaded. 'I think you have been leaned on, told there are security issues here, been ordered to keep your mouth shut?'

Miller stood up and went to the door. He looked flustered. 'I have no idea what you're talking about,' he said producing the same insincere smile he'd devised before.

McCabe wasn't backing off. This young man cared about Segal and that was an emotion which could be exploited. 'Your boss was either attacked by the people who are leaning on you, or they know who did. They didn't tell you it was an attempt on his life, did they? You do want to find the culprits, don't you?'

Jason Miller still looked confused, if not a little frightened. But he was having none of it. He now stood by the door with one hand on the handle. The gesture wasn't lost on McCabe. 'Sorry if you have had a wasted journey, Mr. McCabe. Nice to have met you but I'm afraid, I've nothing more to say.'

Chapter 37

St. Augustine, Florida

The caller to Darlene Shannon was adamant. 'I guess McCabe must have stumbled on something. From our perspective that isn't good. I'd say that is very unfortunate.'

She detected criticism. Perhaps she was being over sensitive. She had the right to be. The caller had always been sceptical about the project, although not alone in that regard. Of course the usual objections had surfaced, regarding feasibility, logistics and danger. At the heart of his protestations was a predictable view about women. No matter how much it was disguised, it was old-school which couldn't consider women competent enough to deal with this type of operation. The rhetoric was usually laced with supposedly flattering remarks about their sensitivity and poise but cloaked in prejudice that was both blatant and insulting.

Shannon thought for a moment. She was determined. It didn't matter what reservations the hierarchy had about this operation; it was going to work, she would make sure it would. She wasn't worried. So, it was unfortunate that a journalist had got a scent; so what? Her caller was overreacting. 'So he's been to see Collins. It doesn't matter. He's an academic. What does he know? It's all theoretical. That's the world he lives in. McCabe has nothing to support the hypothesis of a cloistered intellectual.'

In her heart she wasn't so confident but she made the words sound convincing. However, she would ignore McCabe at her peril. He had a reputation of getting in the way, his journalistic snooping intrusive and dangerous. Even in the US, he'd managed to more than irritate powerful politicos on Capitol Hill, a feat probably unrivalled.

'You know that's not true. I found a transcript of a conference speech he made last month. It's an extract from an academic paper. Wait a moment.'

She could hear the clicking of his computer keyboard in the background. Within a minute he was back on the phone. 'Got it,' he said quickly. 'It's on its way.'

She pulled her tablet towards her and read the text. It was from an obscure academic publication called *Geopolitics*. She scanned the article quickly. There were paragraphs of scholarly discussion, dotted with obscure academic language which meant nothing to anyone outside the field. But there were a few sentences which could easily be consumed by any layperson. It was ominous.

Crime has always been present in Russia, like any other complex society. But what is unique is its development in the aftermath of the demise of the Soviet State. Many of the participants had cut their teeth during their brutal treatment in the Gulags, others were career villains. They all took the opportunities in the chaos and mayhem presented by the dearth of social cohesion and direction. In a word, they exploited the anarchy. Two things, however, have emerged in recent years which are disturbing. On a few occasions there has been a hint of collaboration, if not a dangerous tolerance, between the authorities of the emerging state and this embryonic criminality. It has even been suggested that each one owes the other for its existence. The second alarming trend has been the evidence of Russian criminal activity in Europe. The obvious target for further expansion must be the USA.

Chapter 38

Washington, DC

McCabe stood outside the police headquarters in downtown Washington. The information he'd culled so far was confusing. There were pieces missing, he suspected, which were crucial. The death of Meyer in a stolen yacht had captured the attention of the media, not surprisingly, but their appetites were fickle and momentary. They were easily distracted.

Now Meyer had disappeared from the prominent pages of the local newspaper in Daytona Beach and didn't even feature on the news list of the main newspapers in DC. The Sanchez murder had been given some prominence at the time, primarily because the suspects had been spotted removing his body. The heart attack of the senator wasn't mentioned now either. There was plenty of other hot news in the 'World's Capital'.

Things had gone quiet, too quiet.

McCabe loved Washington in many respects. Other aspects of it he loathed, where power and influence were the currencies, where loyalty was a rare commodity, where the truth was reshaped and remoulded, so it was no longer recognisable. There were influences sufficiently powerful to remove any obstacle. The local police were particularly vulnerable when their job unveiled incidents embarrassing to the Establishment. Sensibly, most who found themselves in the firing line sought refuge by keeping their heads down, so looking after their jobs, families and pensions.

Lieutenant Pat Kovarik, DC Homicide Detective, was no such animal; a brilliant cop who loved his work but hated the political quagmire that Washington increasingly had become. He was a man of little compromise, perhaps too rigid in his ideals for a city which relied on moral flexibility and practical compromise. McCabe took the elevator to the third floor, skipped passed the coffee dispenser noisily struggling to produce anything that could be considered coffee where he saw the familiar disappointed faces of those who stared into their plastic cups. He could see Kovarik, through the glass walls of his partition, at his desk, telephone attached to one ear as he worked behind his usual mountain of paperwork.

He saw McCabe, finished his call and rocked back in his chair to welcome his visitor. 'Well, McCabe, I told you on the phone. These are not my cases.'

McCabe smiled, sat down on a spare chair in front of the detective and placed a carton of freshly made coffee on the desk. The purists would consider this a bribe. He was hoping.

To say the detective loved coffee was an understatement. He'd almost become an addict since forced to give up cigarettes in the wake of new legislation prohibiting smoking in public places and eventually succumbing to the nagging from his wife. His favourite was straight, ordinary coffee with a little milk; no lattes or air-frothed coffee-flavoured bubbles but real coffee he could taste. Kovarik didn't hesitate. He reached out, grabbed the coffee without waiting for an invitation, flipped open the container and took a mouthful quickly.

'OK, McCabe what do you want?'

Forget the sweet talk and the bullshit was the form. Any of that and McCabe would be out the door before he got to the end of his first sentence. They'd known each other for quite a while now but their relationship, if it could be described as such, was unclear. Both hated bureaucracy, the politico-speak of Washington where words had a different meaning to that used by the rest of society but, above all, hated the hypocrisy that often masqueraded as policy. McCabe was here to get any insight he could. This was the detective's baby and he had his finger on its pulse.

But both were inhibited in sharing information, even in a trade. They were supposed to be in opposition; the Press the righteous and champions of the underclasses, and the police the guardians of the law. At least that was the theory taught in universities, where the students had yet to taste the compromises and distaste of the real world.

For his part, Kovarik, hated and distrusted the Press. His job was to catch villains and he was good at it. He also hated anyone who stood in his way. The media he knew had different priorities. They were in search of stories with no price too high. That was his view and he'd take some convincing otherwise. But not for the first time had he used its influence for his own purpose.

It was an interesting balance, both with their reservations but with focused ambitions.

McCabe liked him. He thought Kovarik was one of the good guys.

'You've been busy, McCabe. You're fortunate I didn't send someone to arrest you.'

'Why?'

'Now don't let's get off on the wrong foot. You met Dwight Sanchez a day or so before he was murdered.'

McCabe looked surprised. 'You didn't waste much time in finding that out.'

'It was in the calendar on his cell phone, nothing very clever,' said the detective quickly.

'Surely you don't think I had anything to do with his death?' asked McCabe, sounding genuinely surprised.

Kovarik continued to sup his coffee. 'If I had you'd have been locked up long ago. But it's out of my hands, now.'

'What is?'

McCabe didn't need any further explanation. It was all quite predictable and it had happened to the policeman all too often. On the whole Kovarik loved his job and Washington but occasionally, usually when he ran into the political forces that were stronger than his authority, he hated them both. Mostly it took the form of some meeting with his boss who, happy to bend to authority, would give him a directive. It would be couched in sycophantic superlatives, suggesting that the detective should see the bigger picture. But the message was clear; drop it.

McCabe knew exactly what the policeman's reaction would be. At best, he'd leave his meeting without saying a word. At worst, he'd remind his boss that he was a cop, not a politician. There would be no superlatives, but perhaps the odd expletive, murmured inaudibly under his breath.

Kovarik would be pissed off. 'The case,' he answered sharply. 'It's out of my hands. You know what I'm talking about. Don't fuck with me, McCabe,' he said bluntly.

McCabe smiled to himself. The old warhorse hadn't lost any of his brain cells in his transition to caffeine from nicotine, or his sense of justice and independence. He still held a torch for them against corruption, no matter how subtle. 'It's out of your hands; in whose hands is it now?'

Kovarik shrugged his shoulders. 'Take your pick. I was told to back off. If Sanchez was one of your contacts, my guess is, you know the answer to that question.'

McCabe said nothing.

The detective was still not being drawn. He seemed to be engaged in a personal battle. McCabe knew he was not a man easily persuaded. He knew that Kovarik needed to get where he was going by himself.

'If I had any free hands, they'd be tied behind my back anyway. I can do nothing,' Kovarik repeated, stressing his point. 'But we were at the scene before them,' he said quickly. 'They were too late!'

McCabe looked at him earnestly. Was this dedicated cop, hater of the press, really suggesting what he appeared to be? If this catch was really on the line, he'd have to reel the policeman in ever so carefully. Undoubtedly, this was an invitation.

'Who are they?' McCabe asked cautiously.

Kovarik said nothing. For a moment he just stared at the glass partition. 'What's your interest in Segal?' he asked without any caveat or preliminary remark. He was still struggling with an inner soul. 'We were at his house before anyone else as well,' he added quickly.

McCabe now knew the game they were playing. He was hoping he'd got the rules right.

Kovarik could not and would not tell him anything outright. It would be in code or innuendo.

McCabe had to read what was being said. It was his job to interpret. It was his move next. 'I thought Segal had suffered a heart attack,' he lied, watching the detective's reaction closely.

'Provoked by what?' teased Kovarik. In his own way he was confirming what McCabe already knew; the senator had been attacked, the heart attack was a con.

McCabe was treading even more carefully now. 'Surely you would only have been involved had it been murder or attempted murder?' he asked quietly.

Kovarik smiled as if to confirm the credibility of the question but said nothing. He finished his coffee and impressively lobbed the empty carton into the trash can ten feet away.

McCabe waited for the caveats.

There were none. It was McCabe's move again. 'If I were to surmise there was a connection between those two incidents would I be wrong?' he asked, feeling his way through the conversation.

Kovarik smiled but again said nothing.

'And Sanchez?' pushed McCabe.

'As I said, he was your source, you know the answer to that?'

McCabe thought for a moment. It was unlikely the cop could have got much before the curtain came down on him.

'Fingerprints,' he asked tentatively. It was as good a guess as any.

Kovarik smiled but again said nothing in response. That much was confirmed too.

Once more McCabe could detect Kovarik's inner conflict. He stood up, as one of his team came through the door. 'I'm sorry I couldn't help you, Mr.McCabe,' he said loudly for theatrical effect. 'As I said, they're no longer our cases. Thanks for dropping by.'

Chapter 39

Washington, DC

Kovarik gathered his thoughts as he sat outside the police building and watched McCabe crossing the street. He'd disguised his answers as much as possible, but the journalist was an old campaigner and, in his case, could be led to water. He had no regrets. His job was difficult enough without the political sparring that, for too long, had been accepted practice. He'd refused to be part of that new norm where the power brokers on Capitol Hill could easily exert their authority, stretch a few influential muscles then investigations could be redirected if not stopped.

But his conscience was clear. He hadn't disclosed anything. What he'd directed McCabe towards wasn't easily traced back. He looked around him as he sat on the forecourt, as if the very thought made him a target. He'd given the journalist enough, no more.

A different part of the story had emerged the day before when another body had been discovered in a parking lot behind Union Railway Station. The venue for the crime surprised no one. Although only a stone's throw from Congress, at certain times of the night it would be better advised to avoid the neighbourhood. The bloodied body of a man had been found there in early morning by a night-shift worker collecting his car. It was face down with part of his head several feet away. Homicide had been notified and the detective's team summoned. Initially, there was no indication that the incident was any more extraordinary than the dozens of other random, senseless acts of violence in the city. The corpse had been taken to the forensic lab, as a matter of routine. A witness to the crime, who smelled heavily of drink, when interviewed by the police, claimed he saw two people fighting. Whether the death was the result of that squabble, the witness was unable to establish. Neither were the police.

'It was the tattoos which made me think about it,' the head of forensic had stated. He'd pulled back the cover on the body. Given the condition of the corpse, it was difficult to make out the shapes. The words on the patterns were almost indecipherable.

He produced a book containing different shapes, colours and sizes of tattoos. Some of the artwork was colourful, some in black and white. The designs and figures etched onto the skin whether on the chest, arms or legs, varied enormously, but most had a religious theme. The forensic had flipped through the manual until he found one that vaguely looked like the imprints on the man's arms and shoulders. It wasn't an exact match but it was very close. He pointed to the page and then to the corpse.

'There is slight fading and discoloration through wear and tear but it's definitely that design,' he said confidently.

'So?' asked Kovarik, clearly unimpressed. 'So?' he asked again, impatient.

The forensic looked a little fazed. 'Sorry, I didn't explain the connection.' He pointed to the header on the top of the page. 'No doubt at all,' he said. 'Most of these are classic IDs of ex-gulag inmates, now career criminals.'

'Ex-gulag?' repeated Kovarik. 'What the hell is someone like that doing in Union Station?'

The scientist nodded. 'It's definite. And he stinks of tobacco.'

'So he is a smoker. Well that's definite then. He is a criminal.'

The forensic didn't rise to the bait. He knew that Kovarik, an ex-smoker, had a thing about smokers being marginalised by obsessive politicians, among others. 'I don't know if it tells us anything but this was the only personal effect he had on him,' he said throwing a used packet of Sobranie cigarettes on the table. 'He also reeks of booze.'

Kovarik still looked a little confused. ''Where are we going with this? Why should I be interested in the fact that he is.......'

'Russian,' interrupted the forensic. He paused for a moment. 'And either an ex-political prisoner or more likely a career criminal?' He stopped and let his meaning hit the detective. 'On its own it means nothing,' he added.

'But?' prodded the detective, trying to prise a quick answer.

'It was amazing. I only found it out by chance. I took them, as a matter of routine.'

Kovarik looked ready to scream. 'Are you going to tell me any time soon or are you going to keep this jewel to yourself?'

The scientist smiled with mild satisfaction. He loved a tease. 'His fingerprints match the ones we picked up at the Sanchez murder and in the senator's house. Now, tell me that detail isn't interesting? Also, he may have been killed by someone he knew, if our witness statement is worth anything.'

'What does that mean?'

'There are two of them,' responded the forensic quickly. 'All for the price of one,' he added with snigger.

Kovarik didn't respond to the humour. 'I take it there is no match on the database for his prints?'

The forensic smiled then pulled out another sheet from a folder, looked at the photo mounted on it then studied it from a different angle. 'He had several markings facially but it didn't prevent us getting an ID.' He looked pleased with himself. 'Isn't technology wonderful?'' He pulled out two more photos and inspected them too. 'This is a snap of his passport. Even in that pose he looks menacing.'

Kovarik took the pictures. 'Where did you get these?'

The forensic looked a little smug. 'There are some in this country who would claim privacy issues here. I'm not getting into that argument,' he said sounding a little pompous. 'I'm sure you can do the arithmetic.' He turned over another sheet from the file and read from it 'His name is Vladimir Blatov, Russian, entered the US about a month ago at Dulles Airport in DC, on a diplomatic visa, supposedly part of the Embassy Trade Delegation in Washington; no other information. We have no information on who his friend might be but we're working on it.'

Chapter 40

Washington, DC

He could see the sun setting over the Potomac on one side and the silhouette of the clocktower of Georgetown University on the other. From the veranda of the Kennedy Centre, McCabe could also watch the evening commuter traffic working its way through the trees on the riverbank opposite. The traffic below him on his side of the river was just as busy, as it raced past on its way out of town.

It was still a little chilly as he leaned on the wall and played with the ice cubes in his Black Label. With a little encouragement, the barman had been generous with the whisky. It was a Press function and sometimes the caterers were a little stingy, particularly when serving good quality liquor. Not so this time. He'd smiled appreciatively at the measure and at the barman. That satisfied them both.

On his home ground, back in Washington, he felt a little more comfortable. Even when enjoying the opulent surroundings of a five star hotel and its services, it wasn't quite like home on his houseboat where there was a guaranteed amount of agreeable and familiar disorder. Any he'd manage to create in the hotel in Florida had been tidied by the time he'd returned from his day. It never felt like home.

He walked from the veranda to the Press Reception. Why he was there he wasn't sure. He could be at a function every day if it pleased him. As the Editor-at-Large in the US for the *London Daily Herald* the invitations came to him thick and fast. There were book launches, most of which he'd try and avoid, receptions by some politico or other trying to sell his or her public persona, the standard PR lobbyist soirees selling any ideas their clients were prepared to pay for and the ubiquitous diplomatic bash. Invariably the latter would be at the respective embassy but some ventured into neutral territory, like in this case, by sponsoring some artistic event. The Kennedy Centre for the Performing Arts had been the setting for many such functions, from folk music to opera. Tonight was an opportunity for the Russian Ambassador to host a piano recital by one of his country's most prominent musicians.

McCabe wasn't the best judge of such talent but the brief concert, which had just finished, was magnificent.

But he was here for a very different purpose. Normally, the invitations to events arrived with little ceremony at the downtown DC office. They were filtered by the efficient news desk and then sent to him, if appropriate. A few arrived in his personal email. This invitation to the Kennedy Center had been sent that morning directly to him at the DC office. Since the concert had been arranged several weeks, if not months before, it told him two things. The invitation was last minute and he was a primary target. For what he wasn't sure although the Russian influence, given his recent interest, was too much of a coincidence. Were his enquiries making waves or was it much more? The invitation had the hallmarks of a setup but for what? This was one summons he couldn't refuse.

Washington was a home to hundreds of diplomats, whose job in the time they were in the US capital, was to sell their country and its culture. It was also the venue for international political games, each one as intriguing and devious as the other, each manoeuvre as subtle as the one before, where truth was difficult to unearth.

For those reasons, it was reputed to be one of the most difficult diplomatic gigs on the planet, as the newcomers grappled with the often disturbing overt culture of America. Most of them had been used to subtle exchanges using coded diplomatic-speak but the US had a different style. A lifetime of learning how to interpret coded language seemed redundant as the Americans appeared happiest when talking in plain language without anyone needing to decipher. Too many confused diplomats never made the transition.

McCabe sauntered over to the hospitality bar, smiled again at the attendant while pushing his empty glass forward.

'Mr. McCabe?' said a voice from behind his right shoulder. Nina Vasilev, the Russian Embassy Head of PR, was smiling broadly in her predictably professional fashion.

He'd met her before; an attractive woman but something about her always made him uneasy. She was a powerfully built girl, originally from Bulgaria, and it didn't take too much to imagine her labouring on a farm. He smiled at the thought. He suspected that her entire family was built the same. He was finding it difficult to erase the image. He stepped forward and kissed her lightly on each cheek. 'Nina, how are you?' he asked. 'You look well.' The words were bland but warm, if not a little clichéd. Unwittingly, he was already playing her game.

She smiled. 'Surprised to see you at such an event, Mike,' she said, clearly testing the waters.

It was no surprise to her at all, thought McCabe. The invitation would have come through her office, if not sent by her personally.

'You didn't know I was coming?' he asked mischievously. He thought since he was there he'd have a bit of fun.

But the Russian was no fool and her patriotism had been well tested through years dealing with the western media. She didn't take the bait. 'I think it's about time you wrote a story about Russians in the USA,' she said with no hint of humour. 'We could help you a lot, if that is the type of story which interests you.'

'Really!' he said, feigning some interest.

She was fishing. Her question told him that he'd rattled somebody's cage. It was obvious she'd been briefed but what was the story she'd been given? He'd like to know that too. What she told him was a clue. His questions around town had provoked an interest in certain quarters. Who those people were, provoked another set of questions.

'There have been a lot of changes in our country. America is now a very popular place to visit for Russians,' she said, producing her professional smile again.

He returned the gesture by raising his glass just as the crowd began to thicken around them. 'I'll remember that Nina,' he said politely. 'But I don't write travel pieces. I'm more a hard news man. You know, the stuff people don't want me to print.' He was being really mischievous but he couldn't resist the wisecrack.

She had on her serious face again. The smiling facade had gone and she looked more ready to do battle. 'Perhaps a trip to our country, as our guest of course, would give you a better picture?'

'Flying first class, of course,' he responded. He must stop misbehaving.

'How else?' she responded, almost in reflex.

The fish was on the hook. He pulled hard on the line. 'A cruise ship would be even nicer.'

Her face looked grave. Somehow she didn't like the remark. 'I could be persuaded into doing a piece on Russian cruise ships,' he added, throwing some bloodied flesh into the now shark-infested waters.

'Russian cruise ships?' she repeated then seemed to hesitate. 'You're interested in Russian cruise ships?'

'I've been told they've become very popular with Americans. What do you think?' Now he was fishing.

She faltered a little, as she tried to put an instant answer together. 'I'll need to get back to you on that, Mike,' she said, almost in a whisper. She didn't sound too confident.

He was being really naughty. Now the sharks would be in a feeding frenzy. With a bit of luck, they'd assume he knew more than he did. Perhaps that would produce a result? It was a gamble. He knew nothing and what he did know was superficial. He had the headlines but no story, no substance.

He thanked her graciously for her generosity, took a cracker from the hospitality table, smothered it in caviar then wandered outside to the veranda to enjoy the remainder of the evening. He hadn't found out why he'd been invited. But he'd learned something. His few ripples had made some impact.

McCabe was back on his houseboat in less than half an hour. The evening had produced a positive result in some ways; the whisky was excellent. Embassy events, whoever the generous host, always managed to acquire some of the best booze in town, not unusual since they had the money and influence that guaranteed access. The gantry of scotch at the Russian party contained some of the best he'd seen in a long time, probably since the last Russian do.

Not surprisingly, when he got back, he'd had that warm glow inside, the hallmark of too much alcohol. He'd taken a cab back to the boat; a sensible strategy given what he'd consumed. But his head was clear enough and he'd been thinking, on the journey home, about the few strands he had of the story. But there was still no obvious pattern.

He had a number of positive leads, a few possibilities and a handful of flyers. He was being generous. Most of them were like paper streamers, blowing in the wind with no anchor and even less direction. He was convinced there was a Russian connection but that was vague and the evidence circumstantial. Even if the Russian embassy seemed to show an interest in his activities they appeared unsure how to react to his questioning. Their PR's hesitation could mean anything or nothing.

The Flagler professor had dismissed his assertion of Russian Organised Crime. He'd given him a short social history lesson, cautioned him to be careful but told him precious little else.

And Kovarik? There was no doubt he had confirmed a connection between the Sanchez murder and the attempt on the Congressman's life. What else did the detective know that he wasn't disclosing?

Kovarik didn't need anyone's help to solve his crimes backlog but he was shackled by the politicos who pulled his bosses' strings. Perhaps he expected McCabe to get into places where he could not or, by his very presence, change the rules?

Also, it was evident that Jason Miller, from the senator's office, had been gagged.

In both cases, they begged the same questions; who had the power and why?

Chapter 41

Washington, DC

The morning was fine again; calm had descended over the river. Fresh from the shower with coffee, laced with nothing but cream, McCabe stretched his legs out from his chair on the deck of the houseboat. He had a little fuzziness in his head but given his consumption the night before, he was in good shape. That was undoubtedly a monument to the quality of the booze he'd enjoyed.

He still loved houseboat living, particularly on a morning such as this one. There were plenty of hassles surrounding this lifestyle like ensuring supplies of fresh water, securing efficient plumbing and weatherproofing but he'd got the bug in London and had been determined to do the same when he came to DC. He loved it. There was no landlocked apartment which deprived him of the fresh air on deck and the accompanying views. This was a small urban nautical paradise.

He was so relaxed he hadn't heard the characteristic squeak of the gangway, as it yielded to his visitor's weight. He wasn't even startled when the hand touched him on the shoulder. Sharon Grant seemed to tower over him, as he slouched in his chair.

He smiled. 'You're like the proverbial bus,' he said, pulling himself upright.

She looked puzzled.

'It's an old British phrase. You wait for a bus and two come along at the same time.'

'Really!' she responded, still looking bemused.

'I haven't seen you for such a long time and here we are again in a matter of days,' he explained.

She still looked deadpan.

'Can I offer you a drink?' he said, having struggled to his feet.

She looked at the coffee cup in McCabe's hand. 'I'll have what's in there.'

He shepherded her down the stairs to the lounge, poured her a coffee and another for himself. He sat down opposite on the sofa. 'I don't remember inviting you here,' he said jokingly.

Her expression was still deadpan. 'This is not a social call,' she said earnestly. 'Jason Miller's apartment was burgled.'

'You're not suggesting....'

She put up a hand and shook her head. 'Don't be ridiculous. I think whoever did it was a little fitter than you, Mike; with respect.'

He pulled in his waist a little.

'Also violent; not your scene I think?'

'What? Tell me!'

She gave an account of Miller's attack and the serious wounds he'd suffered to his head and body. 'Hit from behind and beaten repeatedly. Our forensic team believe he interrupted a robbery. We have a couple of neighbour's testimonies which seem to support that. A man was seen running from the house.'

'How is he?'

'He's fine but a little scared. I think he knows more than he's telling,' she said.

McCabe went to the fridge and poured himself a beer.

'Why have you come here to tell me this?' He sounded cynical. He couldn't help it. She was here for a purpose and her agenda wasn't entirely clear. Whatever she was up to, it was likely to be on her terms. That would always be the case. He agreed with her reservations about Miller but why was she here confiding in him? Did she expect him to know the answers to her questions this time? That was more likely than her sharing confidences.

He was getting a little sick of being the stalking horse. 'It's obvious to anyone who has talked to Miller that he is hiding something. I believe he's been gagged,' he said watching her reactions, as he savoured the cold beer. 'Since you're here telling me this, I assume it's not you?'

She didn't look comfortable.

'Was it?' he asked sharply. There was no way to grill her subtly. But she wasn't here to pass the time of day. As he'd already concluded, she had her own agenda, and like Miller she knew more than she would say. Perhaps she was gagged too? He wondered how far he could press her. 'Sharon, why are you here?'

She said nothing, finished her coffee and handed him the empty cup, looking for a refill. 'We went through the CCTV that covers the Senate Building, at least the security entrance.' She took the refill, stared at it for a moment then took a sip. 'Meyer is on a bit of footage from two weeks ago. There are some cameras inside but for some reason we don't have any pictures, not in that area. So, we don't know if he went to see Segal but it's a good bet. That would appear to add another dimension to this murky picture.'

Sadly, the lovely Sharon Grant left. He'd debated a dozen times whether she was his type and vice-versa. They'd always had pleasant times together but there was something missing, certainly on his side. He was sure it was entirely mutual. The essence of it was, neither trusted each other. But he was glad she gave him a lead. It wasn't charity. She had her motive whatever it was. He could only guess. In time he'd find out.

It was a good visit, although, a timely reminder of what his story was about. It had begun with a man, an ex-neighbour, who had been found shot dead on a stolen yacht in Florida. He looked out of the lounge window and could see Meyer's houseboat. It was easy to get distracted.

He meandered along the quayside to one of his favourite fish restaurants. Their breakfast specials were worth the trip. He glanced at the chalked writing on the noticeboard; smoked haddock and poached egg with homemade wholemeal bread; a no brainer. He ordered quickly and sat by the window. The river was a little choppy now and from where he was seated he could see his houseboat tossing about in the waves.

It didn't take him long to devour the breakfast. It lived up to his expectations. His cell phone rang.

Sharon Grant's ID flashed on the small screen. 'I don't know what your plans are Mike, but I thought I'd alert you. Jason Miller has just signed himself out of Georgetown Hospital.' It was obvious what she wanted him to do.

He hailed a cab. 'Senate Building, please,' he said as he slid into the back seat. What the hell, he didn't have any other strategy. Stalking horse or not, he'd go along for the ride.

Chapter 42

Washington, DC

He should have called ahead but he wanted to surprise the young man. McCabe agonised his way through the Senate Building security and made his way to Segal's office. Both desks in the outer office were occupied but there was no sign of Jason Miller.

'He's not here,' said the young woman he'd seen on his last visit, as she interrupted her typing. 'He was attacked at his home last night and was hospitalised,' she said as she pulled off her earphone headset. 'Really sad, but I don't think he's badly hurt. He is home now.' She returned to the dictating machine.

McCabe pulled out his Press Card and waved it in her face. She looked blankly at him.

'I'd like to visit him. It's important. He does know me. I need his address,' he said, not confident she'd respond.

She didn't. She slipped her headset back on and continued to type.

McCabe stood his ground and stared.

After a minute she looked up, now aware he hadn't moved. 'I'm sorry Mr. McCabe,' she said looking at his card again. 'We are not allowed to give out that information.' The headphones went back on.

McCabe gestured to her headgear again.

She pulled them off impatiently. 'Please believe me, I would love to help but that's the office policy. I'm sure you're aware the senator is recovering from a heart attack. It's been left to me to run the office. Sorry!' On went the equipment and she resumed her typing.

He was outside five minutes later more than a little annoyed with his progress or lack of it. The number he'd dialled on his cell phone had trouble connecting. He redialled. Eventually it clicked and began to ring again.

She picked up the call immediately. 'Sharon Grant,' she said.

'Mike McCabe. Twice in one day. Is this another proverbial bus meeting?' she said without a hint of humour.

He ignored the remark. 'Sharon, I need Jason Miller's address. I should have guessed he wouldn't be at work.'

'You should have,' she answered bluntly.

'Well?'

There was a silence. He began to talk to her again. 'His colleagues seemed reluctant to give me any information.'

'I've managed to work that out myself,' she responded curtly.

'Which is why....'

'I get the picture, Mike,' she interrupted.

He was getting impatient. 'Sharon, I don't have time to play these games. Are you going to help me or not?' He was annoyed the words sounded so harsh. But he was pissed off. 'If it's a problem forget it.' He was ready to press the red button. He wasn't in the mood.

'Give me a few moments. I'll text you the address.'

He nodded. 'Thanks.' He hoped it sounded genuine.

The house was small and neat, near Eastern Market Capitol Hill, an area which once was dangerous and unfashionable. In the last few years, the wind of change had blown across this small enclave, which now boasted a village atmosphere, with trendy bars and restaurants. The houses in the neighbourhood were much sought after, the larger ones selling for spectacular sums. There was a time, McCabe remembered, when you couldn't give away some of the property here. There were also small dwellings, with two bedrooms and no basement, built originally for local workers. Miller lived in one.

McCabe pressed the bell gently. Nothing happened. He gave it a little muscle and it screamed out.

Miller got to the door quickly. He stood for a moment without saying anything, left the door ajar and walked back into the house.

McCabe followed.

'I've been expecting you,' he said, standing erect at the far end of the small lounge. 'I should have told the office to give you the address. I guess you had to use your own contacts?' He looked self-assured, as he sat down in an armchair. 'I guess you know I was burgled last night. Unfortunately I walked into the middle of it,' he said, holding the plaster above his eye. The bruising around his face was quite visible with its sickening blue and yellow colouring.

'I'm sorry,' said McCabe, about the same time that a bullet smashed the window and tore a slice off the top of his right arm. He hadn't felt its initial impact or heard a sound as the silencer released its bullet. He then saw the blood ooze from his wound. He felt faint. That was the last thing he remembered until the paramedics began calling instructions to him and then clamping a mask across his face. Then he felt sick and sore. He passed out again.

'Two things are obvious. The shooter was poor or had an off day. Also Miller was the target. Not a surprise then, he's disappeared,' said Darlene Shannon, sitting at the end of the bed.
'Where am I and who are you?' asked McCabe, looking a little groggy.
She studied his face, as if she was considering whether to answer him or not. 'Let's say I've an interest in Harry Meyer too,' she said quietly.
'Enough to be following me around Florida and now DC?' he asked poignantly. Was this the woman Tracy Garrison had warned him about? He remembered her words. *The guy watching you reported to some dame, tall, elegant, sophisticated; not your type, too classy for you McCabe.* He smiled at the recall. 'Your leg man was spotted tailing me. He was also clocked reporting to you; not as inconspicuous as you thought, amateur, if not ham-fisted.' He stopped to see if his words had any effect. He didn't see any. 'Did Harry Meyer report to you as well?'
She still looked cool.

'It cost him his life.' He was trying to provoke her. 'What was he doing for you?' He was still studying her.

She said nothing.

'Smuggling? Was that the story? Harry Meyer was your inside man. Now he's dead.' He was laying it on as thick as he could. There was only a hint of uneasiness as she fidgeted slightly but she wasn't taking the bait. She began to speak. 'I think you're out of your depth Mr McCabe.'

He pulled himself upright in the bed, winced, felt a little breathless but was determined to have his say. 'Who are you to tell me what to do?' he snapped. His shoulder was sore, and he was not in any mood to even attempt being pleasant. 'You walk in here giving me a list of instructions. Who the hell are you and where did you come from?

She didn't flinch for a second. Her self-assurance was impressive. He expected her to respond to his obvious anger and colourful language. She didn't. 'It was just as well we were keeping an eye on you, amateur and ham-fisted though we were, don't you think? Or else you might not be here.'

He backed off, sighed a little and realized he may have overdone the theatricals. 'Sorry,' he said sounding genuine. 'I'd still like to know who the fuck you are?' He laughed, hoping she would see the humour in his comment.

Again, she made no obvious response, no nervous hand gestures, no embarrassing flushes, nothing. This girl was in total charge.

'My name is Darlene Shannon and I work for a branch of national intelligence.'

'Which one?' fired McCabe. The aggression was his instinctive reaction when he was being leaned on; an automatic defensive mechanism. It had no effect on her at all.

'At this stage, I'd rather not say,' she said coolly 'The least you know, the healthier you'll be.'

It sounded patronising to McCabe. He hated it. 'So, you're one of the faceless people who live in the shadows?' he snapped back. He was having trouble being civil. He was determined he wasn't going to concede much ground to her but he could sense her tone was getting more hostile. He could play that game too.

'If you're so smart you'll have worked out that the target was Miller, not you.' She'd drawn first blood.

He conceded the blow with a nod. 'That saves me asking you the question, why me? But I will ask the next obvious one, why him?'

She stood up. Garrison's description of her didn't do the lady justice he thought; she was tall and elegant alright. She was the same woman he'd seen on a CNN report when they'd found Harry Meyer, he was sure. 'I came to see if you were alright. But I'm taking this opportunity to warn you.'

McCabe pulled himself up, as much as he could, given the medical apparatus he had strapped to him. 'I'm used to being given warnings. That's a polite description for a threat,' he said, trying to keep the aggression within acceptable limits.

She smiled in response. 'I would have thought the gunshot wound you suffered would be enough of a warning,' she said and turned to go towards the door.

He was hoping to draw second blood; no chance, he thought. She'd got that too.

'I've read your biog, Mr. McCabe. Be careful, this is not a third world country.' The silence that followed was meant to be dramatic. It was. 'I know you have a lot of courage but there are forces of which you have no experience. The bullet which pierced your shoulder could just as easily have gone through your neck. I'm sure you are more than aware of that.'

Chapter 43

Washington, DC

Kovarik had got a call from the emergency services shortly after they'd arrived at the address of Jason Miller. The call triggered alarm bells in him, as did the description of the man lying on Miller's floor. The police had been alerted by a call from a neighbour who'd heard a shot and the noise of breaking glass. His Press Card ID told them it was Mike McCabe.

McCabe had been unconscious and was in bad shape. The paramedics had him laced up with an oxygen mask and a drip before the policeman had any chance to talk to him. He had lost a lot of blood and the medical team had elbowed Kovarik aside as they pushed him into the ambulance and raced him to the hospital.

Kovarik suspected this was going to be another incident which was taboo. There would be another political cordon thrown around the shooting, he'd be given a directive from his boss to leave well alone and allow the faceless shadows of inland security to deal with the matter.

He didn't have much time.

He hated this subterfuge. It was no secret. His boss knew how he felt. This was his patch yet day after day, he'd be subject to some political interference, some pressure to look the other way. They were policemen, not political appointees subservient to the whims of some US politburo. That was the theory. In the real world, the powerbrokers could exert influence on a whole range of his activities; certainly in this city. But he was no novice. He'd learned to play their game.

He watched as the ambulance took McCabe away then pushed open the door of the small house and joined the rest of his team inside; one from forensic and a junior detective. 'We've got about ten minutes, I guess, before this place is sealed. Pick up anything you can get from that desk,' he said pointing to the corner of the room. 'Check the printer and any pieces of paper that look important. Miller is on the run. Whatever he had someone was prepared to kill for but there is every chance he didn't have time to take it with him.'

Kovarik paced the room, had a quick look in the adjoining kitchen and bathroom. He didn't have to time to check the bedrooms. He looked at his watch. 'OK, guys, time to go. We're out of here; talk to you later.'

He'd just slid into the driving seat of his car. His cell phone rang. The ID was as he expected; his boss. The political waves were already lapping at his shores. 'Yes, sir,' he said nodding into the phone, raising his eyebrows and trying to prevent a frustrated sigh. 'No, we haven't entered the premises. Would you like me to do that?' he asked, almost sarcastically. He knew the answer to that stupid question. 'I'll make sure it is sealed and I'll arrange a uniform presence on the front door.' He nodded into the phone again and managed a middle-finger gesture to the caller.

The results from Kovarik's unofficial raid on Miller's house were disappointing. In the short time they'd been there only two documents of likely importance had been found. One was an official-looking letter with Senator Segal's headed notepaper, which turned out to be a thank-you note and another scrap of paper referring to a future meeting; a useless catch.

The detective looked disappointed as he read the report at his desk. He'd already had another call from his boss, ever frightened of being politically wrong-footed, asking once more for a reassurance that Miller's place had not been entered and had remained as it was when the emergency services had arrived. 'I can tell you no more, sir,' reassured the policeman. 'Everything is as it was,' he said, forcing a smile down the phone again. His boss hung up, a happy man, content that he'd made a significant leap forward in his ambitious ladder-climbing, grovelling, sycophantic strategy.

Kovarik sighed as he turned to the last page of the report and read the attached note.

These poorly focused photos are two of several found on the carpet. They look like the inside of an office. I've improved the image as much as possible but it really is hard to tell what it is.

Kovarik ran his eyes across the photos. So what? It may mean nothing. Attached to it was a list which meant even less. The first column appeared to be the name of equipment, the second the quantity and the third the per unit price. It looked like an invoice but it wasn't made out to anyone. There was no letterhead.

His cell phone rang. He glanced at the caller ID. It was forensic. 'I managed to get the bullet they took out of the journalist shot at Miller's place. I'm running a few checks on it but at first sight I'd say it's from an automatic.'

'Nothing revealing there then?'

The phone went silent for a moment while the forensic seemed to ponder. 'Unless I'm mistaken, it's from an automatic that the police use, as do most of our colleagues in the government agencies.'

'You're not talking about the library service, I guess?' responded Kovarik, in an attempt at humour.

The scientist didn't sound amused. 'You know damn well what I mean and it's not the library service either. It looks as though you haven't avoided the politicos entirely.'

'The Agency, Homeland Security, or whatever the shadows call themselves these days,' commented Kovarik.

'Were they after Miller or the journalist?'

'Could be either. I think McCabe got in the way. Bad luck!' said Kovarik.

'Whoever was the intended target, he's got some powerful enemies,' added the forensic.

Kovarik's face was serious. 'If you're right, he'll need some powerful friends too. This isn't good news.'

Chapter 44

Washington, DC

McCabe was on the mend, at least that's what he'd decided before he tried to drive his car. As he slid behind the wheel, he gasped as the pain on his shoulders took his breath away. 'Fuck,' he shouted loudly as he slipped the key into the ignition.

He was home from the hospital in about half an hour, the slowest drive he'd ever made in his entire life. He could barely move by the time he'd parked. Without too much success he tried to manoeuvre his aching body sideways out of the car. He couldn't do it without nudging something and sending a fresh pain shooting up his arm onto his shoulder. He tried again, cautiously pushing the door open without using his shoulder. 'Damn,' he shouted again as he hit the doorframe on the way out.

He hobbled the remainder of the distance to the boat without incident, after awkwardly manipulating the stairwell into the lounge before collapsing exhausted onto the sofa. The medics had given him a few painkillers with strict instructions to stay off the booze. He hauled himself to his feet and dragged his aching frame to the kitchen and poured himself a large Black Label. He stared at it for all of a minute debating the wisdom of it. He threw it down in one, felt it hit his empty stomach and burn its way to his core. He shivered a little. But it felt good.

He struggled back to the sofa, his eyes drooped in a tiredness that now drained him then he fell into an untroubled sleep. Two hours later he awoke on his side, with a crick in his neck, to add to the biting pain in his shoulder.

Most of the day had gone, as the last of the sun was dipping over the far riverbank. He busied himself making a sandwich and a batch of coffee. He felt a little light-headed still. The food helped.

He hadn't noticed the small envelope on the coffee table. He stretched out, tore the sealing apart and pulled out a blurred photo. He turned it over but there was no indicator what it was or where it had come from. It wasn't there when he'd returned from the hospital. Whoever had delivered it, and it clearly hadn't been the Post Office or a courier service, had done it with some stealth.

He caught a shadow crossing the window above him on deck. He grabbed a bottle of Black Label by the neck. No, that would be a waste of good whisky. Instead, the baseball bat he kept by the stairwell, would suffice. He climbed the stairs quietly. The figure was difficult to make out as it leaned over the front of the boat. McCabe lifted the bat.

'You're not really going to try and hit me with that?' asked Kovarik, spinning round as McCabe got to the top of the stairs.
'I think I would probably have knocked your teeth out by the time you finished the move.'

McCabe, somewhat chastened, if not a little embarrassed, dropped the bat on the deck. 'You'll never know how close you came.......'

'Yep, I never will,' agreed Kovarik.

Five minutes later they were each enjoying a beer in the lounge.

'I'm not supposed to drink,' said McCabe.

Kovarik said nothing. He continued to enjoy his beer.

'I was at Miller's place shortly after the paramedics arrived,' said Kovarik, seated on the sofa.

Opposite him on a chair, McCabe tried to get comfortable. 'I thought you'd been frightened off by your boss and his friends?'

The detective ignored the remark. 'We went into the house before the thought police started leaning on me. Why were you there?'

McCabe shook his head. 'I wish I knew. I was fishing. He's my line to Segal.'

'We picked that up,' the detective said, pointing to the content of the envelope. 'There were several of them on the carpet. It looked as if they came from the printer.'

'What is it?'

Kovarik shrugged. 'My forensic team didn't know. I don't. It looks like a photo taken from a concealed camera, a phone perhaps. It's out of focus.'

'What does it mean?

'It might mean nothing. I'm only the messenger. I am off the case, remember. I hear you've been warned off the case too.'

'How do you know that?' asked McCabe, sounding genuinely surprised, remembering his elegant visitor at the hospital.

Kovarik looked a little smug. 'This is my territory.'

McCabe knew it was a stupid question; the answer was obvious. Kovarik stood up and walked towards the stairs. He hated covert influence but he wasn't being dealt out of this hand. He'd play it his way, albeit with the attached risks. As he got to the stairwell he turned. 'I thought you might like to know that we found a Russian, shot dead at Union Station yesterday. His prints match the ones at the crime scenes of Sanchez and Segal. He's supposedly a trade delegate at the Russian Embassy. Don't ask me what that means. I don't know the answer to that either. But it may explain why the spooks have taken an interest, although what's the chicken and what's the egg?'

Kovarik continued to climb the stairs. 'Before the heavy mob arrived and officially nudged me off this case, we got the slug from your arm.'

'And?'

'From an automatic used by the police and the security boys; now don't you find that interesting? If the shot was meant for Miller, it's no wonder he's on the run. We've got an alert out for him. I'd like to know from him what the hell is going on. We might soon know. That is, if someone doesn't get there first.'

Chapter 45

Washington, DC

Darlene Shannon spread the photographs out on her desk at the Coastal Intelligence headquarters in Washington. They'd been found in Jason Miller's house and passed onto her when she'd arrived there shortly after the shooting.

The project had gone sour. It was no secret that she was focusing on the activities aboard the *Orient Atlantic*. She didn't know the details but enough had emerged to convince her there was something afoot.

She was aware that some colleagues had made no secret of their opposition to her handling of such an operation. She could hear their criticisms echo in her mind. But she'd been determined then to challenge their cynicism and reservations. She felt just as resolute now.

A sequence of events had stalled any progress. She claimed bad luck. Her detractors blamed incompetence. First the brutal murder of Harry Meyer had sent the assignment in a spin. The shooting of Charlie Shepherd, before she had even spoken to him, prevented her making any progress in that area. The steward's first-hand information would have been vital.

Then there was the attempted murder of Jason Miller. His boss Senator Segal had supposedly suffered a heart attack. She was privy to the truth. The congressman had been the victim of a savage assault at his home in Georgetown which had nearly caused his death. Segal was no stranger to security issues and she was confident he knew what had occurred on the cruise liner.

She studied the photos laid out on her desk again. She'd had the photos digitally enhanced and magnified but the results were disappointing and even more out of focus. Had they been perfect, she still wouldn't have known what they meant. The only clue to their importance was that Miller, according to her computer experts, had been printing copies from his computer just before the gunman struck. They were sprayed all over the floor. It wasn't clear what he intended to do with them but he'd had some purpose in mind.

'It was difficult to determine what was important but we checked every file that he had opened just before the shooting,' said one of her investigators. 'He had printed off several of those, for what purpose we don't know. He ran out immediately after the shooting. Both the printer and the computer were still on. The print tray wasn't attached, so the copies sprayed all over the floor. My guess is that at least one is with the police.'

She didn't like that answer. They were having enough difficulty keeping a lid on the project without the intervention of the local police. They had been leaned on before and her security colleagues ensured control but only so much political muscle can be used without third parties getting involved.

In this case, the third party and the shooting casualty were but one; a journalist called Mike McCabe. He wasn't the target but now he was a victim. She knew his pedigree. If he didn't have a cause celebre before, he had one now. Someone shot him; what other endorsement did he need that he was on the right track? She couldn't but admire his single-mindedness but he'd become a major nuisance and he'd grown from being a sideshow to a major event. She'd tried to warn him off at the hospital. But that was a mistake. She should have left it well alone. Things had gone badly wrong.

Harry Meyer, his neighbour, had got him involved intentionally, of that she was now sure. Was that Meyer's guarantee that any untimely death would be investigated?

McCabe stretched out his legs from the bench in the park behind the White House. It was the favourite of those having a quick sandwich lunch, a better option than staying stapled to an office desk. He loved it because of its atmosphere, which allowed him to forget his world and let his thoughts drift away. There was nothing more therapeutic than studying people, their walks, their expressions and guessing their personalities. The urban wildlife added another dimension to the distractions. He opened the brown paper bag by his side and extracted two hot dogs, laced with onions and chilli sauce, purchased from the vendor at the edge of the park; another vital component of his park excursion. He had two large bites; culinary bliss.

It had just begun to rain and, predictably, the park began to empty.

Without saying anything to announce his arrival Jason Miller quietly slipped onto the opposite end of the bench.

McCabe didn't show any surprise but finished his mouthful before he attempted to comment. He looked round the park, inspected the other benches that were occupied, then returned his gaze to his visitor. 'You do know I took a bullet meant for you?' he said gently touching his wounded arm. He had another look around. 'I trust they're not following you to finish the job?' It was meant to be humorous. On reflection, he thought it in bad taste.

The remark didn't help Miller any. He looked far from relaxed. He too was checking every person who moved in and out of the park. He must have inspected the remaining occupants of the benches several times. 'I don't find that funny.'

Neither did McCabe. The humour that had been in his voice earlier had gone. 'Surprisingly, neither do I,' he said quickly. 'Come on, level with me, tell me what the fuck is going on or get the hell out of here. I don't want to find myself in the firing line again.'

Miller slid along the bench, closer to McCabe. 'I don't know the entire story but I'll tell you what I know.'

McCabe looked past him. His eyes caught someone rising from a bench quickly. There was nothing to worry about he concluded. 'You can begin by telling me who shot me. I take it you have no doubt the bullet was meant for you.'

Miller nodded and looked frightened. 'Yes, that's why I ran.'

'You could have helped me,' said McCabe bluntly. 'You ran out on me. I could have been fucking dead.'

Miller shook his head, as if ashamed. It was difficult to tell what he did feel. But he looked troubled. 'I don't know who fired the shot or why.'

'Shit, Miller, it's not fucking nuclear physics. They wanted to shut you up. What is it they don't want you to tell?'

Miller mumbled incoherently. 'That's what so frightening. I don't know anything.'

'They seem to think so; enough to kill you,' replied McCabe bluntly. He was hoping it was crude enough to penetrate Miller's brain. It worked.

Miller looked even more anxious. 'Maybe they just wanted to frighten me.'

McCabe shook his head, as if in despair. 'Well they succeeded admirably on that front. You're scared shitless.'

Miller's head darted to the left quickly to catch sight of a man running from the park. He stepped back and studied another man who'd done the same. He froze as the two men, accompanied by another came walking quickly back into the park. He never said one more word. He was gone.

The three men chased and eventually cornered a small dog which had skipped its lead and was ecstatically enjoying its freedom.

McCabe watched helplessly as the farce unfolded. By now, Miller was out of sight.

Chapter 46

Washington, DC

Nina Vasilev read the memo which had landed on her desk. Her superiors were not happy. They were dissatisfied with the little information she had culled from the British journalist Mike McCabe at the Kennedy recital.

She could imagine the criticism; despite their faith in her and their endorsement of her abilities, she'd disappointed them. She'd let the party down, her family, the country and every other loyalty they could contrive. They knew how to play with her emotions. They managed to engender guilt. That was their style. But she'd learned to live in their world and knew the game they played. She wasn't going to be intimidated.

She shook her head in disbelief. It was she who had put her faith in them, not the other way around. The layers of faceless men above her, she'd never met. What she did know made her cautious, a collection of spineless assholes, few would trust.

They knew her views. Her loyalty was unquestionable but their self-absorption was often blatant and embarrassing. She liked her boss but he was well out of his depth. What he envisaged the PR operation at the Russian Embassy to be, she couldn't imagine. He'd arrived from Moscow, heavy with political recommendations, and military qualifications that allowed him generous latitude. But he was a product of the bureaucratic school of government. That ethos was simple but staggeringly inept; never be in a room when a decision was made and sign nothing. It was obvious he'd lost his nerve and in the last few days he'd become increasingly paranoid.

Washington was not an easy stint and the line between operational security and PR was often invisible. Those, like herself, who were in frontline contact with foreign diplomats and the western Press needed to be on their guard. With their jobs came high expectations.

Since the recital at the Kennedy Centre she had found herself babysitting a neurotic boss. McCabe's oblique references to the cruise ship at the Kennedy recital confirmed he knew something. How much he knew was still uncertain. He either knew nothing or was playing games. By reputation, it could be either. It was naive of her superiors to assume that she could get anything out of him who, notoriously, guarded his information and his sources.

She turned the handle to the office door cautiously and quietly slipped into the room.

Her boss seated at the other end, sheltered behind his desk, looked distressed. He forced a smile. His body language, crouched almost shrinking, gave the impression he was hiding. It was obvious to her that he was under huge pressure with which he was having trouble. She could hear his anxious breathing.

'It was unfortunate that we couldn't get more information from the British journalist,' he said, his hands fidgeting with a

paperclip on the desk. 'And now that he has been shot,' he added, and stopped, hoping the implications would be obvious.
'It would help me, if I knew of our involvement,' she said candidly.
'This has got too messy,' he said wringing his hands nervously, ignoring her enquiry. 'That's the second shooting. The first was the man who died on the yacht,' he continued as he pulled a piece of paper closer to him. 'Meyer, Harry Meyer,' he murmured, as if he didn't want her to hear. 'He was a neighbour of the British journalist which is the reason he has become involved.' His breathing relaxed a little as he looked at her. 'Our people think Meyer had something which he'd taken from the cruise ship,' he said as if trying to unload a terrible burden. 'He may have been trying to give it to McCabe.'
'What was it?' she fired instinctively.

He looked at another piece of paper to his right. He seemed anxious again and his breathing sounded shorter and uneasy, as he leaned across and read from it. 'He spent some time with an American academic at Flagler College in Florida.' He stopped and looked at Vasilev, as if he expected a reaction. He got none. 'I don't know what this is about but apparently the British journalist, McCabe spent some time at Flagler recently.' He was getting increasingly nervous. 'I'm told it's important. That's ALL I've been told,' he emphasised.

She got his point, bent forward to steal a glimpse from his notes, but was unable to read any more. She didn't need to. The look on his face told her the story. It was a directive from on high, a command without any options. It clearly disturbed him.

His eyes ran down the lines of his directive again. 'Meyer's houseboat in DC has been searched without result.' He pulled the paper closer and appeared to read further down the document. 'The Americans conducted one too. I'm informed nothing was found in either search.'

'It's still missing?' she asked quietly, not wishing to add to his anxiety.

'Apparently so,' he sighed, as if he wished the problem would go away.

'What is it?' she prodded again. 'You still haven't told me our involvement in this?'

'I have NOT been told,' he answered quite emphatically. He sounded annoyed that he wasn't in the loop. He appeared increasingly agitated, as he rung his hands endlessly.

She didn't like the direction and tone the conversation had taken.

Her boss was in serious meltdown. 'I've also been told the document may have got into the hands of a US congressman, Senator Segal. Meyer visited him. The implication is obvious.'

She had her own sources. Senator Segal was reported to have had a heart attack. According to her information that was bullshit. The congressman had been viciously attacked; an attempt made on his life at his house in Georgetown. Whoever did that was as stupid as they were crude.

'One of Segal's aides, Jason Miller, acquired the document. The journalist Mike McCabe inadvertently got in the way of a bullet meant for him.' He sighed in despair again. 'Too messy; this is all too messy.'

Chapter 47

Orient Atlantic, East Coast, Florida

The *Orient Atlantic* had dropped anchor just off the northeastern Florida coast, about thirty miles north of St. Augustine. Darlene Shannon, on board a Coast-Guard cutter, had her binoculars focused on its deck. There was little activity now, some two hours after it received a delivery from the mainland. She had her cell phone tuned into a team of Coast-Guard Commandos who had been waiting for weeks to get into action. Shannon had briefed the leader earlier in the day. 'We have a suspicion of what's going on. We think it's trafficking of some description. However, we have no definite proof. We need to get some and fast.'

A few miles away, two delivery trucks had unloaded their cargo onto a large sailing yacht which then sailed to the anchored liner. Boxes were lifted aboard quickly by a team ready for the shipment. It was all over in minutes.

Two BMWs accelerated past the now empty trucks as they made their way from the coast. A mile later, the road curved forcing the truck drivers to slow down. They turned the bend to be met by the same two BMWs blocking the road. A dozen men, armed with machine guns emerged from behind the cars as the trucks slowed down. For a moment, one began to accelerate then appeared to have second thoughts. They both came to a halt, all guns behind the cars focused on the drivers.

Shannon's cell phone rang within five minutes.

'There's nothing in the trucks that'll give us any clue. No markings, no empty boxes,' reported the commando leader.

'What do they know?'

The commando leader looked over at the four scared young men under his guns. He fired several questions at them in Spanish. He got an immediate response. One, who appeared to be their leader, and spoke far from fluent English, gabbled some form of explanation. The story was predictable. They had been paid to pick up several boxes from a warehouse and deliver them to the quayside. The boxes were taken on board a yacht and they got paid by one of the crew.

'They claim they do jobs like this regularly. They get a phone call, pick up the stuff in their own trucks and get paid on delivery,' said the commando down the phone. 'They've no idea what was in the load; all plain cardboard boxes, unmarked. That's the story.'

Shannon didn't like the answer. It told her nothing, at least little more than she'd already guessed. 'Prepare a plan. We need to go in tomorrow,'

'Yes, ma'am, will do. I'll get it to you by tonight. I'll check out the warehouse where they made the pick-up but I doubt it'll tell us anything. They claim there was nothing else there.'

Darlene Shannon stood on the deck of the *Orient Atlantic* watching her team come aboard. Storming the ship with her commandos wasn't the proper approach. Instead from her Coast-

Guard cutter, she'd informed the captain that his ship was under surveillance and would be inspected by a team of professionals, who would board the vessel immediately. She went with the initial wave and gave her credentials to the first officer, a Rumanian, who apologized on behalf of his absent captain. 'He is unable to welcome you on board, personally, Commander. We will give you every cooperation,' he said in perfect English, with a slight hint of west coast America. It was obvious where he'd learned his English.

'I must insist he be present,' demanded Shannon. 'It is his ship and he is responsible for everything on board,' she added bluntly. 'I need to see him now. Please take me to him.'

The officer hesitated.

'Now!' she shouted.

He still didn't move.

'Hold him here,' she directed to the commando by her side.

'Come with me,' she said to the leader of her team.

It didn't take them long to find the captain's cabin but nearly five minutes before they realized that no persuasion would be effective.

She ordered the door be smashed in.

The captain, despite his protests, in what dialect she wasn't sure, was clearly destroying documents in a shredder.

The guns of Shannon's commandos, pointed in his direction, seem to convince him to stop.

Shannon stepped forward. 'Your behaviour would suggest to me that you are complicit in an activity aboard this vessel which you know to be irregular, if not illegal.'

He continued to shake his head vigorously. The babble that emerged could have been in any language. They didn't understand the words but the sentiment was obvious.

'I think you and your crew were also complicit in the murder of this man,' she said, showing him a photo of Harry Meyer.

Now the captain looked really frightened. He shook his head even more vigorously. Another torrent of incomprehensible gibberish erupted. The captain was very upset.

She produced another photo. 'I want you to see this,' she said brandishing an out of focus picture. He looked at it, very confused.

'You have two options. You can show me it yourself, or I'll tear this floating crate apart until I find it. If I have to do that, you'll be lucky to ever see it again. Do I make myself clear?' She didn't really need an answer. She got none.

The commando leader reappeared after an inspection into the depth of the ship. He looked unhappy. 'Ma'am, you had better come and see this. There is a problem.'

Chapter 48

Washington, DC

His laptop was slower than usual or at least its internet connection. One downside of living on the water, in this part of the world's capital, meant that sometimes communications with the rest of the planet weren't great. McCabe shook his head in disbelief.

To be fair, it didn't happen every day. Even the best of networks needed a day off.

The databases he'd been trawling weren't as responsive either.

The Segal name and his assault had been running around his head for days, like keywords in a computer search. But it wasn't the senator's heart attack; something else. He couldn't place the context. It may mean nothing but it was nagging him incessantly.

At last he found it. He had the story on screen.

In the report, Segal was commenting on the death of a fellow congressman. In his own politico-speak he was challenging the medical diagnosis of his colleague's heart attack. The newspaper article was equally ambiguous, listing the athletic activities pursued by the dead man who had a reputation for being one of the fittest senators in Congress.

McCabe checked the name against a couple of databases, and copied the emerging information onto his cell phone. Another piece of software gave him an address and the best route to navigate to it. It was a far cry from his cub-reporter days when he would have needed a dozen phone calls, a telephone directory and a good road map to get this far.

He sat in his car reading the screed on his cell phone. Senator Andrew Howard was a close friend of Segal. Although representing different states and not always agreeing on policy, privately they were very close. Both had been lawyers in their earlier careers, latterly both showing interest in national security. McCabe's news antennae were beginning to bristle. He did another trawl in the database but there was nothing more, save a comment from Segal's wife, which echoed his scepticism.

The small house, on Capitol Hill, at the end of the street where he was parked, was twee, almost as if designed by a child. It couldn't have had more than two bedrooms and had no garden but it was the DC home of the late Congressman Howard.

McCabe closed the car door quietly, climbed the three steps to the front door and was about to knock when it opened quickly. A well-dressed woman in her sixties looked startled but recovered quickly. 'You're earlier than I expected. I haven't the parcel ready.'

He smiled. 'Not me, ma'am,' he said quickly. 'My apologies, Mrs Howard, my name is Mike McCabe,' he said as he showed her his Press Card. The words sounded flat and his presence intrusive. He hadn't felt that way for a long time. 'I'm doing a story about Senator Segal. I know he and your husband were friends. Can I ask you a few questions?' The words seemed to echo in the hallway. They sounded bland.

Her smile was generous. She stepped back from the door and nodded. 'Please do come in. We'll go into the garden.'

He followed her, aware of what he wanted to ask her but unsure of the subtlety of doing it. To revisit her grief was what he was asking her to do. He was having second thoughts about the approach, not to mention the ethics. He felt he had no choice. Two colleagues, who were also close friends and interested in the same issues, supposedly, had heart attacks within a month of each other; that made him feel uneasy. He hated coincidences. His news antennae made little allowance for such occurrences. There had to be an explanation.

There was a definite elegance to her as she sat on a basket chair and clasped her hands on her lap. She gave him her disarming smile again. 'I've heard of you, Mr. McCabe,' she said graciously.

He felt slightly embarrassed.

'My husband was an avid reader and consumed newspapers by the dozen every day. He mentioned many writers from the media quite frequently.'

It was a very subtle and tactful response, he thought.

'Thank you.' He felt just a little awkward.

'You're after a story,' she said, as a young girl entered the garden from the house carrying a tray of what looked like cold drinks. 'It's cold soda water with ice and lemon.'

He tried to look enthusiastic but she detected his hesitation. 'I can offer you something stronger, if you prefer.'

He smiled, as he shook his head. 'No thanks, the soda will do nicely.'

'There was no foul play, you know. It was just one of those things,' she said as she handed him a glass. 'Although, he never had heart trouble.'

She then disappeared into a world of her own, talking about her husband and his work. It was going to be difficult to interrupt her. It was clear her life revolved around her husband and there was a huge gap in her life now that he was dead.

She talked about his passions, his obsessions and his casual interests. They all amounted to the same thing; public service. 'I don't think he was given enough credit for the work he has done.'

McCabe was trying not to be cynical; politicians were not among his favourites. The senator was obviously one of the good guys.

It was difficult to keep her on track. But he'd no intention of interrupting her now. 'His library is a monument to that dedication.'

Suddenly he was alert. The casual small talk had now taken a different turn. 'In what way?' he asked quickly.

She was smiling with pride now. 'He kept everything; correspondence from his constituents, notes, ideas, sometimes transcripts of interviews.' She laughed out loud at what she was thinking. 'He was a human scavenger. I used to tell him that,' she added then fell silent, lost in her memories again.

'Everything?' prompted McCabe.

She chuckled again. 'Just as well we had an attic, otherwise we would have needed to move.'

McCabe was aware he'd have to tread carefully now. Was she exaggerating or was there really a Klondike of congressional secrets in her attic or did it just seem like that to a house-proud women, irritated by mountains of paperwork cluttering her home? There was only one way to find that out; only one question he wanted to ask now. It was a long shot but what did he have to lose? 'Could I see his library?'

She suddenly appeared cautious. 'Why?' she fired at him.

Now she had him on the back foot. He tried to choose his words with some caution. He didn't want to intrude on her privacy or to appear to disbelieve her. 'I would like to see what interested him, particularly at the time of his death.' The explanation seemed banal but he was convinced no other approach would work. 'I'm sure you know that my work depends on information I get from others, people who are willing to share what they know.' The words sounded just as banal. He was hoping the sentiment sounded convincing.

It seemed a long time before she answered his question. 'He was certainly dependable. He made huge personal sacrifices.' She was down memory lane again.

He needed to get her back.

'The library,' he said quietly. 'I think I'd like to see his library.'
He waited again.

She wasn't a person to rush decisions, certainly not in this case. Her pondering seemed to take an unusually long time. He wasn't going to press her, although every instinct in him was desperate for a result. She ignored his impatient fidgeting and eventually spoke. 'I'd be happy for you to do so. The room hasn't been touched.' She stopped talking for a moment then added. 'It has to remain that way.'

McCabe followed her to a small room which overlooked a patio with doors into the garden. He was impressed. It would be a comfortable place for anyone to work, a world removed from the mayhem that surrounded the congressman in his daily life.

'He needed a sanctuary, a place where only he and his thoughts were allowed to abide,' she said as if she was leading a conducted tour.

McCabe had learned not to interrupt her; the more lucid the better.

She was relaxed and unquestionably proud of her husband and his work. She gestured towards the book-lined walls then to the desk. 'This was part of his world, the place where he did most of his thinking.'

He moved towards the desk and sensed her immediate tension. He stepped back and smiled.

'Sorry, I don't feel that I can allow you to go through his papers, Mr McCabe. I haven't gone through them myself,' she said politely.

'I understand,' he replied, unable to disguise his disappointment.
She continued her conducted tour.
McCabe tried to look interested but her commentary was predictable. He was trying his best to read the content of some of the papers lying on the desk but without success. His attempts hadn't gone without notice.
'Perhaps, when I've had time to go through them, I'll publish some, if it's appropriate,' she said softly.
It was clear he wasn't getting easy access to this Klondike; certainly not today, if at any time. As he walked away from the desk, he spotted it, resting on top of a printer to the left of the desk. It didn't look as if it was part of the congressman's collection, perhaps just a flyer dropped through his letterbox that he'd picked up from the doormat. With his back to her he moved towards it.
Her attention was elsewhere.

Five minutes later he was seated in his car outside. He wasn't happy with himself. It was another five minutes before he pulled out the brochure from under his coat. He couldn't resist taking it; a leaflet with a clear picture of the *Orient Atlantic* printed on the top.
He turned the flyer over to read the handwritten scrawl on the back.

They're scared. They've been scared since the cold war started. They got neurotic when the cold war ended. Then they didn't know who or where to point, so they could blame somebody or something when things went wrong. After nine-eleven they were adrift. All the great moral platitudes that had taken root during Nixon's time were jettisoned. You remember them? The ones formed after it was found he'd been using government agencies to spy on fellow Americans. Yes, after nine-eleven all bets were off. That's the real world now, they said. The US had long decided that being a spectator was lethal. Of course, that's not for public consumption. The French, the British, the Swedish, the Danish, the Dutch, they've all learned that lesson. They're singing from the same song sheet.

I know it doesn't make it right. We'll throw away the Constitution, the Bill of Rights and we could even chuck in the Ten Commandments. They talked about people getting hurt and this piece of warped logic is going to save us all. I know you said we'd be no better than they are; does that matter? I've decided I can't go along with it.

Chapter 49

Washington, DC

McCabe had read and reread the scrawl on the back of Howard's brochure. There was no evidence to suggest that it referred to the cruise ship. Perhaps it was the draft of a speech about a different subject entirely. Somehow he didn't think so but he didn't have any worthwhile theory that might explain the text.

He had an idea about some aspects of the story but there was nothing hard. He was convinced that Meyer was on an undercover operation, one that clearly went wrong. And who was pulling his strings?

The ubiquitous presence of Darlene Shannon in Florida and now in DC gave him an unexpected clue. A few phone calls established that she was a highly ambitious mover working for Coast Guard Intelligence. It was a good bet she was Meyer's boss.

He had the impression she wasn't chasing a few smugglers either. The stakes would appear to be much higher. She'd also ordered his surveillance.

Undoubtedly the *Orient Atlantic* was at the heart of this affair. There seemed to be so many traits to the story. It began to take a different shape depending from which angle it was viewed. There appeared to be a Russian connection but somehow it seemed too obvious, too clumsy, too contrived. A Russian organised crime racket was dismissed by Collins, the Flagler professor, although he hadn't totally dismissed the suggestion that there could be a connection.

Kovarik's input suggested that there were manoeuvres in the shadows, particularly with the discovery of a murdered Russian at Union Station.

There was no correlation between any of these singular events; certainly none that he could see.

He'd been told by Shannon to back off from his investigations. That meant he was causing a disturbance. The same had been told to Kovarik.

It meant instructions were being sent from the political twilight zone to stop them.

And what of Segal, his supposed heart attack and his terrified assistant Jason Miller? The young man's last attempt at conveying what he knew was a failure, as successful as his previous one. On both occasions he'd run at the slightest threat to his safety. He could hardly be blamed, given what had happened to his boss. He was not one of life's lions.

Was he just one of those bystanders who innocently found themselves sucked into something of which they had no knowledge and over which they had no influence? Perhaps Irina, the Russian-American girl and her friend Charlie Shepherd were two more, desperate to remain aloof from the turmoil around them, but unable to do so?

And of course there was Harry Meyer, his one-time neighbour, whose murder aboard a stolen yacht in Florida, had triggered the story in the first place.

McCabe looked back at the Howard's brochure and read the scrawl yet again. Was it a speech or a collection of thoughts that was never meant to be shared with anyone? There was only one source who could answer those questions; Viktor Segal.

McCabe turned right when he emerged from the elevator, passed two hospital check-in desks and was then confronted by a uniformed policeman outside the senator's room. Not surprisingly, the security was tight. Segal was conscious now, sitting up in bed. Given what he'd gone through, he looked in good shape.

'Mr. McCabe, we meet at long last. Not in the best of circumstances. I got your message. I'm happy to talk to you but I'm not sure I can help.'

He was surprised at the negative reaction, although he really had no reason to think otherwise. If the influences which leaned on Kovarik and on Miller were anything to go by, the pressures were coming from a world peopled by the likes of Segal. The congressman would disclose nothing, unless his life depended on it.

But McCabe didn't want an argument with a heart patient at the side of a hospital bed.

Suddenly Segal looked past him.

McCabe turned quickly to see the uniformed policeman confront what looked like a white-coated doctor at the door. The figure pulled out a gun and in the same movement hit the policeman across the face. The uniform collapsed, as the figure pushed his way into the room.

McCabe stared at him and the gun, about six feet away.

The gunman moved forward towards the senator.

Instinctively, McCabe stood in his way. He didn't know why. Segal was stretching for an alarm button on the drawer unit at the side of the bed. He didn't get that far. A bullet from the gun silencer barely made any sound as it tore into the pillow at the top of the bed.

Unwittingly, McCabe had forced the gunman to alter his line of fire.

Suddenly, Sharon Grant came through the open door. Her left elbow caught the gunman in the small of his back. He turned quickly to face her, still holding the gun. Fearlessly, she moved forward, and kicked the gunman in the groin. He screamed. McCabe winced. He could feel the pain from where he was standing.

The gunman's legs collapsed and he was on his way down. He'd barely got half way to the floor when he met her right knee. His nose and teeth took the full impact.

McCabe heard the crack. What had broken he couldn't determine. He couldn't decipher one damaged part from the other. The lower section of the face was covered in blood, as the gunman sank the remaining distance towards the floor. Her right hand chopped into the back of his neck, just to complete the manoeuvre. She stood over him, kicked away the gun which had landed on the floor, and inspected her handiwork. He was out cold. He wasn't going anywhere, anytime soon.

The speed of her professionalism didn't surprise McCabe. The choreography was impressive. She hardly looked as if she'd broken sweat. She was beside the senator in seconds, checking to see if he'd been injured by any ricochet.

'Who is he?' asked McCabe, moving towards the body.

Grant stood in his way. 'There no need for you to go any further,' she said gently holding his arm. 'Mike, that's far enough.'

She didn't resist when he pushed her aside. 'The SOB nearly killed your boss and would have been happy enough to kill the rest of us. I'd like to know who he was and why?'

She moved again to block him. 'It's better you don't know any more about this,' she said quietly.

'You know, I'm fucking sick of people telling me that it's better that I don't know,' said McCabe, aware that she could dispatch him with the same efficiency she did the man on the floor, who was slowly gaining consciousness. 'In my world that means back off and mind your own business. Well, you'd better get used to the idea, I'm here for the duration and I'm going to get to the bottom of this.'

Two uniforms arrived and walked towards McCabe.

Grant shook her head and nodded towards the intruder on the floor.

They dragged him to his feet, unsympathetic to his bleeding face, handcuffed him and bundled him out of the room.

'Mike, I think it is best left to another time,' she said pointing to the door. 'You'd better go.'

Chapter 50

Washington, DC

He'd made little impact on Sharon Grant. Retreat appeared the only option. By the time he got back to the parking lot his head was swimming.

McCabe put the key in the ignition, automatically checked the rear-view mirror and screamed. 'Gees, what the fuck?' he shouted. The driver's window was open and two groups walking to their cars stared immediately in his direction. He dropped his head on the steering wheel. He finished his sentence. 'What the fuck are you doing in my car? You scared the shit out of me.'

'Sorry, there was no other way. I had to make sure no one saw me. I parked at the far end of the lot and made my way here on foot.' Jason Miller looked extremely distressed. 'They're targeting me; I know they are.'

'Slow down. Tell me who they are and what's going on?'

Miller looked over his shoulder through the back window of the car then scanned the parking lot in every direction.

McCabe's nerves were in tatters. He was badly in need of a drink.

The young man seemed to relax after his survey. He didn't see anything that seemed to make him more nervous. 'I have to tell someone. I did try before but it wasn't the right time.'

'What about now. I've just witnessed another attempt on your boss' life. '

'No, please don't tell me that?' replied Miller with obvious despair in his voice.

'A gunman managed to get past his security guard and a police cordon and shot him.'

'Oh, no, no,' replied Miller, almost choking. 'They got him, after all. I knew they would.'

'They didn't,' said McCabe quickly, still staring through the rear-view mirror.

Miller's body seemed to deflate as he sank into the back seat. 'Thank God,' he sighed. 'But they'll get him. I know they will.'

'Tell me what the fuck is going on,' insisted McCabe. His neck was beginning to get sore by watching Miller in the mirror.

'Drive me to my car at the back of the lot. It's a little red Nissan.'

Miller jumped into the passenger seat beside McCabe. 'I've only managed to put the pieces together myself from what I've uncovered.'

'You didn't discuss it with Segal then?'

'It was difficult, as you'll find out. But I did locate some notes he'd made. They were handwritten notes in one of his cabinets. They outlined some of the details.' Miller told him about getting into Segal's cabinet with the code. He started to ramble but in the midst of his obvious fear was a story.

McCabe took out his notebook and tested his shorthand again. Whether he'd ever be able to read it back was another issue. He'd soon find out.

The essence of the tale was simple but bizarre. Apparently, in one of Segal's discussions about the legal constraints imposed on the CIA only being able to operate outside the USA, he'd mooted the idea of the cruise ship.

'I know Segal; it was a joke. The FBI and other Homeland agencies patrolled the mainland.'

'Why?'

Miller's speech was faltering a little as he tried to be coherent. But he was seriously stressed. 'Increasingly, there were those in the Agency who didn't like the constraints. The idea went from a joke to a serious proposition. Some in the Agency loved the idea; a floating offshore base from where the Agency could influence the political game.'

'What do you mean by that?' fired McCabe immediately.

'The media, the opinion makers; some in the Agency were sick of the liberal voice.'

'I still don't follow you.'

Miller looked even more nervous, if not slightly embarrassed.

'The Senator wasn't being serious.'

'Yes, you've told me that already. I still don't know what you're saying.'

Miller looked even more uncomfortable. He had another inspection of the parking lot. Satisfied, he relaxed again. 'There were some who wanted to do it for real.'

'You're still haven't told me what you mean. Spell it out!' McCabe was shouting now. Whatever patience he'd had with Miller had just run out. He'd told him nothing. It was a meaningless ramble. He looked at the notes he taken and sighed.

Miller sensed the mood. 'Across one floor, on the lower deck of the *Orient Atlantic*, they'd set up a huge room with dozens of computers, manned by young Agency operators. They'd been ferrying the equipment in for months. That's what gave the game away. Hence the need for the cover stories.'

'How could they do that?'

'Money, money; that's how. I doubt if the owners of the ship knew anything about it. All possible with an amenable captain.'

'To do what?'

'You would recognise it immediately. It was a newsroom.'

McCabe closed his eyes in disbelief. 'You mean a FAKE newsroom?' he said, emphasising the word.

'Strictly speaking it was a genuine newsroom but the news was fake,' corrected Miller. He smiled for the first time. He seemed to see something humorous in that part of the story.

McCabe's face showed his feelings. Clearly, he didn't share the humour. 'You're kidding me?' he said, shaking his head in disbelief.

'They had hundreds of different accounts and names on social media which the Agency operators used.'

'Spewing out propaganda?'

'A lot more. This was an alternative media operation, totally controlled by a security agency. Where have we seen that model before?'

'So, this was a permanent operation?'

'Initially, it was just meant as an experiment, like a piece of research. I suspect that's how they got the funding and diverted the prying eyes inside the Agency. But they became more ambitious, as they saw the results. They were going to test things here to be used, who knows where?'

'Doing what?'

Miller had his usual nervous reconnaissance of the parking lot then settled down again. 'They had fake accounts on Facebook, Instagram, and Twitter by the dozen.' He stopped and appeared to get more nervous. 'They had facsimile front pages of every major newspaper across the globe, in several languages.'

'Surely they'd be discovered?'

'Sometimes but the idea was also to cause chaos, uncertainty.' Miller began to ramble again.

Once more McCabe tested his shorthand. It was a rogue Agency outfit, unbridled, which considered such an operation necessary in an America now dominated by a liberal media, continued Miller. When anyone came close to discovering the operation, they'd laid it at the door of dope smugglers or Russian organised crime. They were prepared to kill to keep the secret.

The picture was getting disturbingly clear. 'These people believed they were fighting a war. They were on the front line.

Segal found they had affiliations across the globe, particularly Europe. It is scary.'

'And where did Harry Meyer fit in?'

'The Agency used the Coast Guard. A very ambitious woman called Shannon headed their Intelligence operation.'

'I know, I've met her.'

'The smuggling suspicion was an Agency ruse to prevent the true purpose being discovered.'

'But Shannon wasn't stupid. She couldn't nail it but she knew there was something not right. It didn't ring true even for a smuggling racket. So, she set up her operation. It was elaborate. She was determined. They stole a yacht from St. Augustine harbour to tail the *Orient Atlantic* and to discover what was really going on. Meyer was an old hand at that game. He took it and had been watching the cruise ship for more than a year. But he was no fool either and he knew eventually he had to go on board. That's when it went sour.'

Miller kept looking about him, surveying the parking lot again, taking a deep breath and then trying to continue before he started the routine again.

'I don't know when he first did it but Meyer contacted the senator. He knew his interest in security. It was ironic that it had been his idea in the first place.'

'What did he tell him?'

'I don't know but I have been through his papers.'

'And?'

'All that surfaced were a few notes of his meeting with Meyer, outlining the smuggling and Russian smokescreens, and a blurred photo. I think Meyer used his iphone to take a shot of the newsroom on the *Orient Atlantic* and sent it to Segal. The picture just looks like a photo of a large insurance room unless you knew the context.'

'And there have been a number of people looking for it ever since?'

'Is that why Meyer was killed?' asked McCabe quickly. He wanted to get to the core before Miller dried up on him.

Miller shook his head. 'By now the Russians had become aware that they were the fall guys. The Russians leaned on anyone who could tell them what was going on and the Agency people were going to silence any leaks. Take your pick.'

'Meyer was shot and an attempt made to kill Segal?'

McCabe scribbled a few notes into his book again. 'The Georgia?'

'Ironically, that was one they'd taken to follow the cruise ship.'

'What about the innocents abroad; Irina Lukin and Charlie Shepherd? They had nothing to do with any of this, did they?'

Miller became distraught again. 'The ship had to operate as a normal cruise liner, otherwise it wouldn't work. The Agency had leased a private deck. They had their own security on board but somehow it went wrong.'

'Lukin and Shepherd found out about it?'

'The girl was a hooker and the boy a steward. Meyer told the senator what was going on. That's also in the notes I managed to steal'. Miller began to get visibly distressed again. 'They'll get him. He knows it all. It's a rogue operation but the Agency will close ranks. It will; it must. I don't know about the Ruskies.'

'And what happened to Shannon and the Coast Guard operation?'

Miller shook his head. 'The Agency knew that the game was up. They cleared the place. No one would find anything. Only the witnesses were then the danger.'

'What of Shannon?'

Miller smiled. It was a cynical smirk. 'She's ambitious. She'll get promoted into silence. It works every time.'

'And you; where does that leave you?' McCabe asked quietly. 'You and Segal, are the only people who know about this are you not?' The words seemed to hang in the air. He wished he hadn't said them. They were more than alarmist and certainly not the right words for the occasion.

'And you,' said Miller staring at McCabe. 'And you!' He made his point forcefully.

A car pulled up quickly beside them. McCabe looked round and checked the driver. An old lady petted her dog and got out of a small Chevy.

Miller was spooked immediately, was out of the car and into his own in seconds.

By the time McCabe had turned back, the small red Nissan was screaming out of the parking lot.

Twenty minutes later, relieved, McCabe pulled up outside his houseboat. He raced along the pontoon, up the gangway; first stop the booze cabinet. He could see his hands visibly shaking as he poured himself a whisky. His nerves had taken a pounding in the last hour.

Within minutes he was on his second Black Label. His hands were still shaking.

Chapter 51

Washington, DC

Kovarik looked through the two-way glass mirror into the cell. He checked a photo in his hand of the man seated at the table. It was difficult to tell from the frames taken from the CCTV at Union Railway Station. He was the same size and shape. The face had the same contours but the picture was dark.

Kovarik reckoned he would have about half an hour before the thought police arrived and prevented him from doing anything else. His uniformed patrolmen had delivered the prisoner, as instructed, from the hospital after the Segal shooting.

He was to be held incognito. The detective smiled when told. Not likely, he said to himself. Perhaps he'd just have time to get an inkling of what was going on.

He passed another uniform, guarding the cell. He opened the door quietly and studied the man at the far end of the room. His face was badly bruised, complemented with serious cuts above both eyes. He looked a little the worse for wear.

Kovarik sat in a chair opposite and stared at him. He produced the CCTV photo and lined it up beside the suspect's face. It was him alright. He was the man who appeared to have killed his partner in a fight in Union Station. On the night in question, they were both likely to have been heavily intoxicated and fought over something trivial. One of them died in that brawl, shot over nothing at all. The victim wouldn't know what hit him and the homicidal friend probably didn't realize what had happened until much later.

The detective studied the tattoo chart, given to him by his forensic specialist. The suspect had similar markings on his bare arms, two quasi-religious symbols that had apparently become the hallmark of ex-gulag inmates, now killers for hire. His dead partner's fingerprints were matched against those taken at the Sanchez murder and at the time of Vicktor Segal's attack.

Kovarik's cell phone rang. He listened carefully, studying the Russian all the time. He finished the call, stared at his prisoner then checked his watch. He was running out of time. The phone call was positive but it did complicate matters. The forensic team had just matched the fingerprints of the suspect to both crime scenes too.

Kovarik leaned across the table to the Russian. He spoke very slowly, not entirely sure if he would be understood. 'You killed your friend at Union Railway Station, a man called Sanchez and tried to kill an American senator today, whom I believe you had attempted to kill before. Have you anything you would like to say to me?'

The Russian signalled with his fingers that he would like a cigarette.

The detective sympathised. He'd only recently kicked the habit but still missed it terribly. 'I don't smoke,' he said, trying not to sound sanctimonious. 'But I'll get you one, if you tell me what I want to know.'

The Russian stared straight ahead.

'Who hired you? Who paid you money to kill?'

Kovarik wasn't getting much response. 'Your friend is called Vladimir Blatov, who entered the US on a diplomatic visa, a month or so ago. Soon we'll know your name too.'

'I also,' said the Russian.

'You also what?' asked Kovarik.

'I also diplomat,' he said in his staccato English. 'No need to answer questions,' he said politely.

'Who told you that?'

'Person told me.'

'The person who hired you? From the Embassy?'

The door opened and the uniform guard walked to the table and slid a sheet of paper in front of Kovarik. The detective whispered something to him. The guard shuffled in his pocket for a moment, produced a packet of cigarettes, pulled out two then handed them to Kovarik.

The Russian watched the gesture with his eyes firmly on the cigarettes.

The detective glanced at the note. 'Stepan Blatov,' he said, not quite certain what he'd read. 'You killed your own brother?' said Kovarik, in complete disbelief. 'What kind of low life did they hire here?' the detective murmured. It was quite audible. Over the years he'd experienced almost every abomination known to man. He didn't think he'd be shocked. But he was. The brothers were ex-gulag guns for hire. Perhaps on that drunken evening, their fraternal rivalry was out of control? He handed a cigarette to the prisoner and signalled the uniform to light it.

The Russian took a huge draw on the cigarette, inhaled and seemed to hold his breath for an inordinately long time. At last he exhaled then dropped his head into his hands. It was the end of any dialogue.

Kovarik slowly rose from the table and made his way to the door. At the exit he looked back. Yes, he was sure he was right. Within a half hour the thought police will have arrived and, backed by his boss, a gagging order on any further questioning would be in force. The Russian would probably be on a plane to Moscow the next day.

He pulled out his cellphone as he left and dialled a number from his directory. It was always strange why stories like the Russians, camouflaged and protected by all the government bullshit, found their way into the Press. A mystery.

Chapter 52

Washington, DC

The driver of the red Nissan was not paying attention, as he approached the crossing. A truck with a heavy load of steel girders, raced towards the intersection. Some witnesses would say that the driver of the truck should have taken more care. Others claimed that the small car was going much too fast. The result was the same; a fatal accident in which a young assistant to a US senator was killed instantly. No one mentioned the fact that, immediately after the collision, the driver of the truck got out of his cab, walked to the Nissan, inspected the crushed car and its bleeding inmate then, without raising any alarm, walked away from the scene, casually lit a cigarette and disappeared. The stolen truck was found abandoned at the scene.

.

After a few scotches, McCabe couldn't remember how many, he switched on the television to catch any report on the Segal shooting. He was still unnerved by what he'd seen at the hospital, followed by the traumatic time with Miller. He flipped through the major news outlets. There was nothing. This time he poured himself a double.

He was trying to attach some reason to what he'd just experienced. Were Segal and Miller really targets? On the surface, there appeared to have been attempts on their lives and those of several innocent people. Two had succeeded; Harry

Meyer and Charlie Shepherd. Irina Lukin was still fighting her corner. Miller's story still sounded fanciful. Perhaps it was all coincidence?

He was going over in his mind how he could tell the story. There were still gaps but the major thrust of the tale, Harry Meyer's death, could be explained by an undercover operation gone wrong.

There was a call from Kovarik on his voicemail; no message. He'd give him a call back.

Suddenly he was aware of an unusual silence on the television, as the news reader checked an item which had just come up on his screen. He alerted the viewers to a news flash.

Senator Segal, Democrat Congressman from Virginia, has died suddenly from a heart attack while in Georgetown University Hospital. It was the second he had suffered in a week. The senator died about an hour ago. A spokesman for the hospital said it was totally unexpected.

Series Titles

WHITE COLLAR OPTION

THEN GO STRAIGHT FORWARD

WAITING FOR THE STORM TO PASS

THEIR WILL BE DONE

POINTED INWARDS

MADE TO ACCOUNT

CHAIN REACTION

CONSIGNMENT

TRUE WIND

Bill Johnstone's novels are available in ebook format from Amazon, Apple and Smashwords.

Paperback through Amazon, Barnes and Noble (US) and all major book retailers.

Printed in Great Britain
by Amazon